THE RING
OF THE NIBLUNG

The Rhinegold : Prelude
The Valkyrie : First Day of the Trilogy
Siegfried : Second Day of the Trilogy
The Twilight of the Gods : Third
Day of the Trilogy

First published 2022
Copyright © 2022 Aziloth Books

All Rights Reserved. No part of this publication may be reproduced, stored in a retrieval system or transmitted in any form or by any means, electronic, mechanical, photocopying, recording, scanning or otherwise, except under the terms of the Copyright Licensing Agency Ltd, 90 Tottenham Court Road, London, W1P 0LP, UK, without the permission in writing of the Publisher. Requests to the Publisher should be via email to: info@azilothbooks.com.

Every effort has been made to contact all copyright holders. The publisher will be glad to make good in future editions any errors or omissions brought to their attention.

This publication is designed to provide authoritative and accurate information in regard to the subject matter covered. It is sold on the understanding that the Publisher is not engaged in rendering professional services.

British Library Cataloguing in Publication Data

A catalogue record for this book is available from the British Library

ISBN-13: 978-1-913751-17-3
Cover Illustration:
Donner, The Thunder God
Arthur Rackham (1910)

Raging, Wotan rides to the rock ...
Like a Storm-wind he comes!

THE·RHINEGOLD
& ·THE·VALKYRIE

BY·RICHARD·WAGNER
WITH·ILLUSTRATIONS
BY·ARTHUR·RACKHAM

TRANSLATED·BY·MARGARET·ARMOUR
LONDON · WILLIAM·HEINEMANN
NEW·YORK · DOUBLEDAY·PAGE·&·C°
1910

CONTENTS

The Rhinegold
- first scene
- second scene
- third scene
- fourth scene

The Valkyrie
- the first act
- the second act
- the third act

ILLUSTRATIONS

Plate 1	"Raging, Wotan Rides to the rock! Like a storm-wind he comes!"	3
Plate 2	The frolic of the Rhine-Maidens	12
Plate 3	The Rhine-Maidens teasing Alberich	20
plate 04	"Mock away! Mock! The Niblung makes for your toy!"	24
Plate 5	"Seize the despoiler! Rescue the gold!	26
Plate 6	Freia, the fair one	32
Plate 7	"The Rhine's pure-gleaming children Told me of their sorrow"	40
Plate 8	Fasolt suddenly seizes Freia and drags her to one side	45
Plate 9	The Gods grow wan and aged at the loss of Freia	48
Plate 10	Mime, howling. "Ohé! Ohé! Oh! Oh!"	51
Plate 11	Mime writhes under the lashes he receives	54
Plate 12	Alberich drives a gold and silver-laden band of Niblungs	58
Plate 13	Horrible dragon, O swallow me not! Spare the life of poor Loge!	65

Plate 14	"Hey! Come hither, And stop me this cranny!"	78
Plate 15	"Erda bids thee beware"	81
Plate 16	Fafner kills Fasolt	84
Plate 17	"To my hammer's swing Hitherward sweep Vapours and fogs! Hovering mists!"	86
Plate 18	"The Rhine's fair children, Bewailing their lost gold, weep"	89
Plate 19	"This healing and honeyed Draught of mead Deign to accept from me." "Set it first to thy lips"	97
Plate 20	The likeness between Siegmund & Sieglinde	100
Plate 21	Sieglinde prepares Hunding's draught for the night	105
Plate 22	"Siegmund the Wälsung Thou dost see! As bride-gift He brings thee this sword"	115
Plate 23	Brünnhilde	118
Plate 24	Fricka approaches in anger	122
Plate 25	Brünnhilde slowly & silently leads her horse to the cave	127
Plate 26	"Father! Father! Tell me what ails thee? With dismay thou art filling thy child!"	130
Plate 27	Brünnhilde stands for a long time dazed and alarmed	138
Plate 28	Brünnhilde with her horse, at the mouth of the cave	143
Plate 29	"I flee for the first time And am pursued Warfather follows close .... He nears, he nears, in fury! Save this woman! Sisters, your help!"	158
Plate 30	"There as a dread Dragon he sojourns, And in a cave Keeps watch over Alberich's ring"	163
Plate 31	The ride of the Valkyries	169
Plate 32	A Bridle Fire brighter than ever yet burned for Bride!	178
Plate 33	"Appear, flickering fire, Encircle the rock with thy flame! Loge! Loge! Appear!"	180
Plate 34	The sleep of Brünnhilde	182
Plate 35	End Plate	183

THE RHINEGOLD

CHARACTERS
GODS: WOTAN, DONNER, FROH, LOGE
NIBELUNGS: ALBERICH, MIME
GIANTS: FASOLT, FAFNER
GODDESSES: FRICKA, FREIA, ERDA
RHINE-MAIDENS: WOGLINDE, WELLGUNDE, FLOSSHILDE

SCENES OF ACTION
I. AT THE BOTTOM OF THE RHINE
II. OPEN SPACE ON A MOUNTAIN HEIGHT NEAR THE RHINE
III. THE SUBTERRANEAN CAVERNS OF NIBELHEIM
IV. OPEN SPACE AS IN SCENE II.

FIRST SCENE
At the bottom of the Rhine

A greenish twilight, lighter above than below. The upper part is filled with undulating water, which streams respectively from right to left. Towards the bottom the waves resolve themselves into a mist which grows finer as it descends, so that a space, as high as a mans body from the ground, appears to be quite free from the water, which floats like a train of clouds over the gloomy stretch below. Steep rocky peaks jut up everywhere from the depths, and enclose the entire stage. The ground is a wild confusion of jagged rocks, no part of it being quite level, and on every side deeper fisures are indicated by a still denser gloom. Woglinde circles with graceful swimming movements round the central rock.

Woglinde	Weia! Waga!
	Roll, O ye billows,
	Rock ye our cradle!
	Wagala weia!
	Wallala, weiala, weia!
Wellgunde *From above.*	Woglinde, watchest alone?
Woglinde	If Wellgunde came we were two.
Wellgunde *Dives down to the rock.*	How keepest thou watch?
Woglinde *Swimming off, eludes her. They playfully tease and chase one another.*	Wary of thee.

Flosshilde *From above.*	Heiaha weia! Ho! Ye wild sisters!
Wellgunde	Flosshilde, swim! Woglinde flies: Help me to hinder her flying.
Flosshilde *Dives down between* *the two at play.*	The sleeping gold Badly ye guard; Watch with more zeal The slumberer's bed, Or dear you'll pay for your sport!

They swim asunder with merry cries. Flosshilde tries to catch first the one, then the other. They elude her, and then combine to chase her, darting like fish from rock to rock with jests and laughter. Meanwhile Alberich climbs out of a dark ravine on to a rock. He pauses, still surrounded by darkness, and watches the frolic of the Rhine-Maidens with increasing pleasure.

Alberich	Hey, hey! ye nixies! Ye are a lovely, Lovable folk! From Nibelheim's night Fain would I come, Would ye be kind to me.

The maidens, as soon as they hear Alberich's voice, stop playing.

Woglinde	Hei! Who is there?
Wellgunde	A voice! It grows dark!
Flosshilde	Who listens below?

They dive down and see the Nibelung.

Woglinde and Wellgunde	Fie! the loathsome one!

The Frolic of the Rhine-Maidens

Flosshilde
Swimming up quickly.
Look to the gold!
Father warned us
Of such a foe.

Both the others follow her, and all three gather quickly round the central rock.

Alberich   You above there!

The Three Rhine-Maidens   What wouldst thou below there?

Alberich
Do I spoil sport
By standing and gazing here?
Dived ye but deeper,
Fain the Niblung
Would join in your frolic and play.

Wellgunde   He wishes to join us?

Woglinde   Is he in jest?

Alberich
Ye gleam above me
So glad and fair!
If one would only
Glide down, how close in my arms
Fondly clasped she would be!

Flosshilde
I laugh at my fears:
The foe is in love.

Wellgunde   The amorous imp!

Woglinde   Let us approach him.

She sinks down to the top of the rock, whose base Alberich has reached.

Alberich   Lo! one of them comes!

Woglinde   Climb up to me here!

Alberich
Climbs with gnome-like agility, though with repeated checks, to the summit of the rock. Irritably.

> Horrid rock,
> So slippery, slimy!
> I slide and slip!
> My hands and feet vainly
> Attempt to hold on
> To the slithery surface!
> Vapour damp
> Fills up my nostrils—
> Accursed sneezing!

He has got near Woglinde.

Woglinde
Laughing.

> Sneezing tells
> That my suitor comes!

Alberich
He tries to embrace her.

> Be thou my love!
> Adorable child!

Woglinde.
Escaping from him

> Here thou must woo,
> If woo me thou wilt!

She swims up to another rock.

Alberich
Scratching his head.

> Alas! not yet caught?
> Come but closer!
> Hard I found
> What so lightly thou didst.

Woglinde
Swims to a rock lower down

> Deeper descend:
> Thou'lt certainly seize me!

Alberich
Clambers down quickly.

> Down there it is better!

Woglinde

> But better still higher!

Darts upwards to a higher rock at the side.

Wellgunde and Flosshilde
Laughing

Ha! ha! ha! ha! ha! ha!

Alberich

How capture this coy,
Elusive fish?
Wait for me, false one!

He tries to climb after her in haste.

Wellgunde
Has sunk down to a lower rock on the other side.

Heia! my friend there!
Dost thou not hear?

Alberich
Turning round.

What? Didst thou call?

Wellgunde

Be counselled by me:
Forsake Woglinde,
Climb up to me now!

Alberich
Climbs hastily over the river-bottom towards Wellgunde.

Thou art more comely
Far than that coy one;
Her sheen is duller,
Her skin too smooth.
But thou must deeper
Dive to delight me!

Wellgunde
Sinking down till she is a little nearer him.

Well, now am I near?

Alberich

Not near enough.
Thine arms around me
Tenderly throw,
That I may fondle
Thy neck with my fingers,
And closely may cling
To thy bosom with love and with longing.

Wellgunde

Art thou in love?
For love art thou pining?
Approach and show me

	Thy face and thy form. Fie! thou horrible Hunchback, for shame! Swarthy, horny-skinned Rogue of a dwarf! Find thou a sweetheart Fonder than I!
Alberich *Tries to detain her by force*	I may not be fair, But fast I can hold!
Wellgunde *Swimming up quickly to the middle rock.*	Hold firm, or I will escape!
Woglinde and Flosshilde *Laughing.*	Ha! ha! ha! ha! ha! ha!
Alberich *Angrily calling after Wellgunde*	Fickle maid! Bony, cold-blooded fish! Fair if I seem not, Pretty and playful, Smooth and sleek— Hei! if I am so loathsome Give thy love to the eels!
Flosshilde	What ails thee, dwarf? Daunted so soon? Though two have been wooed, Still a third waits thee, Solace sweet Fain at a word to grant!
Alberich	Soothing song Sounds in my ear! 'Twas well I found Three and not one! The chance is I charm one of many, Whilst, single, no one would choose me! Hither come gliding, And I will believe!

Flosshilde
Dives down to Alberich.

How senseless are ye,
Silly sisters,
Not to see he is fair!

Alberich
Hastening towards her.

I well may deem them
Dull and ill-favoured,
Seeing how lovely thou art!

Flosshilde

Sing on! Thy song,
So soft and sweet,
Entrancing sounds in my ear!

Alberich
Caressing her with confidence

My heart burns
And flutters and fails,
Flattered by praises so sweet!

Flosshilde
Gently resisting him.

Thy grace and beauty
Make glad my eye;
And thy smile refreshes
My soul like balm
She draws him tenderly towards her.
Dearest of men!

Alberich

Sweetest of maids!

Flosshilde

Wert thou but mine!

Alberich

Wert mine for ever!

Flosshilde
Ardently.

To be pierced by thy glance,
To be pricked by thy beard,
To see and to feel them for aye!
Might thy hair hard as bristles
Flow ever more
Enraptured Flosshilde wreathing!
And thy form like a frog's,
And the croak of thy voice—
O could I, dumb with amaze,
Marvel forever on these!

Woglinde and Wellgunde
Dive down close to them and laugh.

Ha! ha! ha! ha! ha! ha!

Alberich
Starting in alarm.

Wretches, dare ye thus scoff?

Flosshilde
Suddenly darting away from him.
She swims up quickly with her sisters.

A suitable end to the song.

Woglinde and Wellgunde
Laughing.

Ha! ha! ha! ha! ha! ha!

Alberich
In a wailing voice.

Woe's me! Ah, woe's me!
Alas! Alas!
The third one, so dear,
Does she too betray?
O sly and shameful
Worthless and dissolute wantons!
Live ye on lies
Alone, O ye false nixie brood?

The Three Rhine-Maidens

Wallala! Wallala!
Lalalelai leialalei!
Heia! Heia! ha! ha!
Shame on thee goblin,
Scolding down yonder!
Cease, and do as we bid thee!
Faint-hearted wooer,
Why couldst not hold
The maid, when won, more fast?
True are we,
And troth we keep

They swim apart hither and thither,
now lower, now higher,
to provoke Alberich to give chase.

With lovers when once caught.
Grasp then and hold;
Away with all fear!
In the waves we scarce can escape.
Wallala!
Lalaleia! Leialalei!
Heia! Heia! Ha hei!

Alberich	Fiercely within me
	Passionate fires
	Consume and flame!
	Love and fury,
	Wild, resistless,
	Lash me to frenzy!
	So laugh and lie your fill—
	One of you I desire,
	And one must yield to my yearning!

He starts chasing them with desperate energy. He climbs with terrible agility, and, springing from rock to rock, tries to catch one maiden after another. They keep eluding him with mocking laughter. He stumbles and falls into the abyss, and clambers up quickly again and resumes the chase. They sink down a little towards him; he almost reaches them, but falls back again, and once more tries to catch them. At last he pauses out of breath, and, foaming with rage, stretches his clenched fist up towards the maidens.

Alberich	If but this fist had one!

He remains speechless with rage, gazing upwards, when he is suddenly attracted and arrested by the following spectacle. Through the water a light of continually increasing brilliance breaks from above, and, at a point near the top of the middle rock, kindles to a radiant and dazzling golden gleam. A magical light streams from this through the waves.

Woglinde	Look, sisters!
	The wakener laughs to the deep.
Wellgunde	Through the billows green
	The blissful slumberer greets.
Flosshilde	He kisses the eyelid,
	Making it open;
	Bathed in splendour,
	Behold it smiles,
	Sending, like a star,
	Gleaming light through the waves.
The Three Rhine-Maidens	Heia jaheia!

The Rhine-Maidens teasing Alberich

Swimming gracefully round the cliff together.

Heia jaheia!
Wallala la la la leia jahei!
Rhinegold!
Rhinegold!
Radiant delight,
How glorious and glad thy smile,
Over the water
Shooting effulgence afar!
Heia jahei!
Heia jaheia!
Waken, friend!
Wake in joy!
That we may please thee,
Merry we'll play,
Waters afire,
Billows aflame,
As, blissfully bathing,
Dancing and singing,
We dive and encircle thy bed!
Rhinegold!
Rhinegold!
Heia jaheia!
Heia jaheia!
Wallala la la la heia jahei!

With increasing mirthful abandonment the maidens swim round the rock. The water is filled with a glimmering golden light.

Alberich
Whose eyes, strongly attracted by the radiance, stare fixedly at the gold.

What is it, sleek ones,
That yonder gleams and shines?

The Three Rhine-Maidens

Where dost thou hail from, O churl,
Of the Rhinegold not to have heard?

Wellgunde

Knows not the elf
Of the famed eye golden
That wakes and sleeps in turn?

Woglinde

Of the star resplendent
Down in the depths
Whose light illumines the waves?

The Three Rhine-Maidens *Together*	See how gaily We glide in the glory! Wouldst thou also Be bathed in brightness, Come, float and frolic with us! Wallala la la leia lalei! Wallala la la leia jahei!
Alberich	Has the gold no value Apart from your games? It were not worth getting!
Woglinde	He would not scoff, Scorning the gold, Did he but know all its wonders!
Wellgunde	That man surely The earth would inherit Who from the Rhinegold Fashioned the ring Which measureless power imparts.
Flosshilde	Our father told us, And strictly bade us Guard with prudence The precious hoard That no thief from the water might steal it. Be still, then, chattering fools.
Wellgunde	O prudent sister, Why chide and reproach? Hast thou not heard That one alone Can hope to fashion the gold?
Woglinde	Only the man Who love defies, Only the man

	From love who flies Can learn and master the magic That makes a ring of the gold.
Wellgunde	Secure then are we And free from care: For love is part of living; No one would live without loving.
Woglinde	And least of all he, The languishing elf, With pangs of love Pining away.
Flosshilde	I fear him not Who should surely know, By his savage lust Almost inflamed.
Wellgunde	A brimstone brand In the surging waves, In lovesick frenzy Hissing loud.
The Three Rhine-Maidens *Together.*	Wallala! Wallaleia la la! Join in our laughter, Lovable elf! In the golden glory How gallant thy sheen! O come, lovely one, laugh as we laugh! Heia jaheia! Heia jaheia! Wallala la la la leia jahei!

They swim, laughing, backwards and forwards in the light.

Alberich *His eyes fixed on the gold, has listened attentively to the sisters' rapid chatter.*	Could I truly The whole earth inherit through thee? If love be beyond me My cunning could compass delight?
In a terribly loud voice.	Mock away! Mock! The Niblung makes for your toy!

Mock Away! Mock! The Niblung makes for your toy!

Raging he springs on to the middle rock, and clambers to the top. The maidens scatter, screaming, and swim upwards on different sides.

The Three Rhine-Maidens	Heia! Heia!heia jahei!
	Save yourselves!
	The elf is distraught!
	Swirling waters splash
	At every leap:
	The creature's crazy with love!
	Ha! ha! ha! ha! ha! ha! ha!

Alberich — Still undismayed?
Reaching the top with a last spring. — Go, wanton in darkness.
Water-born brood!

He stretches his hand out towards the gold.

My hand quenches your light;
I tear the gold from the rock;
Forged be the ring for revenge!
Bear witness, ye floods—
I forswear love and curse it!

He tears the gold from the rock with terrific force, and immediately plunges with it into the depths, where he quickly disappears. Sudden darkness envelops the scene. The maidens dive down after the robber.

The Three Rhine-Maidens   Seize the despoiler!
Rescue the gold!
Help us! Help us!
Woe! Woe!

The water sinks with them. From the lowest depth Alberich's shrill, mocking laughter rings up. The rocks are hidden by impenetrable darkness. The whole stage from top to bottom is filled with black waves, which for some time appear to sink even lower.

Seize the Despoiler! Rescue the Gold!
Help us! Help us! Woe! Woe!

SECOND SCENE

The waves have gradually changed into clouds which, becoming lighter and lighter by degrees, finally disperse in a fine mist. As the mist vanishes upwards in light little clouds an open space on a mountain height becomes visible in the dim light which precedes dawn. At one side Wotan with Fricka beside him both asleep, lie on a flowery bank. The dawning day illumines with increasing brightness a castle with glittering pinnacles which stands on the summit of a cliff in the background. Between this and the foreground a deep valley is visible through which the Rhine flows.

Fricka
Awakes; her gaze falls on the castle, which has become plainly visible; alarmed.

Wotan! My lord! Awaken!

Wotan
Continuing to dream.

The happy hall of delight
Is guarded by gate and door:
Manhood's honour,
Power for aye,
Rise to my lasting renown!

Fricka
Shakes him.

Up from deceitful
Bliss of a dream!
My husband, wake and consider!

Wotan
Awakes and raises himself slightly. His glance is immediately arrested by the view of the castle.

The walls everlasting are built!
On yonder summit
The Gods' abode
Proudly rears
Its radiant strength!
As I nursed it in dream

	And desired it to be, Strong it stands, Fair to behold, Brave and beautiful pile!
Fricka	While thou rejoicest, Joyless am I. Thou hast thy hall; My heart fears for Freia. Heedless one, hast thou forgotten The price that was to be paid? The work is finished, And forfeit the pledge: Hast thou then no care for the cost?
Wotan	My bargain well I remember With them who built the abode. 'Twas a pact tamed them, The obstinate race, So that this hallowed Hall they have built me. It stands—the strong ones' doing:— Fret not thou, counting the cost.
Fricka	O laughing, insolent lightness! Mirth how cruel and callous! Had I but known of thy pact, The trick had never been played; But far from your counsels Ye men kept the women, That, deaf to us and in peace, Alone ye might deal with the giants. So without shame Ye promised them Freia, Freia, my beautiful sister, Proud of playing the thief. What remains holy Or precious to men Once grown greedy of might?

Wotan
Calmly.

From such greed
Was Fricka then free
Was Fricka then free
Herself when the castle she craved?

Fricka

I was forced to ponder some means
To keep my husband faithful,
True to me when his fancy
Tempted him far from his home.
Halls high and stately,
Decked to delight thee,
Were to constrain thee
To peaceful repose.
But thou hadst the work designed
Intent on war alone;
It was to add
More to thy might still,
To stir up to tumult still fiercer
That built were the towering walls

Wotan

Wouldst thou, O Wife!
In the castle confine me,
To me, the god, must be granted,
Faithful at home,
The right to wage war
And conquer the world from without.
Ranging and changing
All men love:
That sport at least thou must leave me.

Fricka

Cold, hard-hearted,
Merciless man!
For the idle baubles,
Empire and sway,
Thou stakest in insolent scorn
Love and a woman's worth!

Wotan

When I went wooing, to win thee
I staked ungrudging,
Gladly one of my eyes:
What folly now then to scold!

	Women I honour Beyond thy desire! I will not abandon Frei, the fair: Such never was my intent.
Fricka *Anxiously looking towards a point not on the stage.*	Then succour her now: Defenceless, in fear, Hither she hastens for help!
Freia *Enters as if flying from someone.*	Help me, sister! Shield me, o brother! From yonder mountain Menaces Fasolt: He comes to bear me off captive.
Wotan	Let him come! Sawest thou Loge?
Fricka	To this tricky deceiver O why wilt thou trust? He always snares thee anew, Though from his snares thou hast suffered.
Wotan	I ask for no aid Where simple truth suffices; But to turn the spite Of foes to profit, Craft and cunning alone Can teach, as by Loge employed. He whose advice I obeyed Has promised ransom for Freia: On him my faith I have fixed.
Fricka	And art left in the lurch. The giants come. Lo! hither they stride: Where lingers now thine ally?
Freia	Where tarry ye, my brothers,

	When help ye should bring me,
	Weak and bartered away by my kin?
	O help me, Donner!
	Hither! Hither!
	Rescue Freia, my Froh!
Fricka	Now the knaves who plotted and tricked thee
	Abandon thee in thy need.

Fasolt and Fafner, both of gigantic stature, enter, armed with stout clubs.

Fasolt	Soft sleep
	Sealed thine eyes
	While we, both sleepless,
	Built the castle walls:
	Working hard
	Wearied not,
	Heaping, heaving
	Heavy stones.
	Tower steep,
	Door and gate
	Keep and guard
	Thy goodly castle halls.
Pointing to the castle.	
	There stands
	What we builded,
	Shining fair
	Beneath the sun.
	Enter in
	And pay the price!
Wotan	Name, Workers, your wage.
	What payment will appease you?
Fasolt	We made the terms
	That seemed to us meet.
	Hast thou forgot so soon?
	Freia, the fair one,
	Holda, the free one—
	The bargain is
	We bear her away.

Freia the fair one

Wotan
Quickly.

Ye must be mad
To moot such a thing!
Ask some other wage;
Freia I will not grant.

Fasolt
Stands for a space speechless with angry surprise.

What is this? Ha!
Wouldest deceive?—
Go back on thy bond?
What thy spear wards
Are they but sport,
All the runes of solemn bargain?

Fafner

O trusty brother!
Fool, dost now see the trick?

Fasolt

Son of light,
Light, unstable,
Hearken! Have a care!
In treaties keep thou troth!
What thou art
Thou art only by treaties,
For, built on bonds,
There are bounds to thy might.
Though cunning thou,
More clever than we:
Though we once freemen,
Are pledged to peace,
Cursèd be all thy wisdom;—
Peaceful promises perish!—
Wilt thou not open,
Honest and frank
Stand fast by a bargain once fixed.
A stupid giant
Tells thee this:
O wise one, take it from him!

Wotan

How sly to judge us serious
When plainly we were but jesting!
The beautiful Goddess
Light and bright—
For churls what charm could she have?

Fasolt	Jeerest thou?
	Ha! how unjust!
	Ye who by beauty rule,
	Proud and radiant race!
	How foolish, striving
	For towers of stone,
	Woman's love to pledge—
	Price of walls and of halls!
	We dolts, despising ease,
	Sweating with toil-hardened hands,
	Have worked, that a woman
	With gentle delight
	In our midst might sojourn
	And ye call the pact a jest?

Fafner	Cease thy childish chatter;
	No gain look we to get.
	Freia's charms
	Mean little;
	But it means much,
	If from the Gods we remove her.
	Golden apples
	Ripen within her garden;
	She alone
	Grows the apples and tends them.
	The goodly fruit
	Gives to her kinsfolk,
	Who eat thereof,
	Youth everlasting.
	Sick and pale,
	Their beauty would perish,
	Old and weak,
	Wasting away,
	Were not Freia among them.
Roughly.	From their midst, therefore,
	Freia must forth!

Wotan	Loge lingers long!
Aside.

34

Fasolt   We wait for thy word!

Wotan   Ask some other wage!

Fasolt   No other: Freia alone!

Fafner   Thou there, follow us!

Fafner and Fasolt press towards Freia. Froh and Donner enter in haste.

Freia   Help! Help from the harsh ones!

Froh   To me, Freia!
Clasping Freia in his arms.
To Fafner.   Back, overbold one!
                                    Froh shields the fair one!

Donner   Fasolt and Fafner,
Confronting the giants.   Have ye not felt
                                    With what weight my hammer falls?

Fafner   What means thy threat?

Fasolt   What wouldst thou here?
                                    No strife we desire;
                                    We want but our due reward.

Donner   Oft I've doled out
                                    Giants their due:
                                    Come, your reward is here
                                    Waiting, full measure and more!
He swings his hammer.

Wotan   Hold, thou fierce one!
Stretching out his spear between   Nothing by force!
the combatants.   All bonds and treaties
                                    My spear protects;
                                    Spare then thy hammer's haft!

Freia

Woe's me! Woe's me!
Wotan forsakes me!

Fricka

Can such be thy thought,
Merciless man?

Wotan
Turns away and sees Loge coming.

There comes Loge!
Hot is thy haste
Smoothly to settle
Thy sorry, badly-made bargain!

Loge
Has come up out of the valley in the background.

What is this bargain
That I am blamed for?—
The one with the giants
That thou thyself didst decide?
O'er hill and o'er hollow
Drives me my whim;
House and hearth
I do not crave.
Donner and Froh,
They dream but of roof and room:
Wedding, must have
A home in which to dwell,
A stately hall,
A fortress fast.
It was such Wotan wished.
Hall and house,
Castle, court,
The blissful abode
Now stands complete and strong.
I proved the lordly
Pile myself;
In fear of flaws,
Scanning it close.
Fasolt and Fafner
Faithful I found;
Firm-bedded is each stone.
I was not slothful
Like many here:
Who calls me sluggard, he lies!

Wotan Cunningly
Thou wouldst escape!
Warned be, and wisely
Turn from attempts to deceive.
Of all the Gods
I alone stood by thee
As thy friend,
In the gang that trusted thee not.
Now speak, and to the point!
For when the builders at first
As wage Freia demanded,
I gave way only,
Trusting thy word
When thou didst solemnly promise
To ransom the noble pledge.

Loge Perplexed to puzzle,
Plans to ponder
For its redeeming—
That promise I gave;
But to discover
What cannot be,
What none can do,
No man can possibly promise.

Fricka See the treacherous
Rogue thou didst trust!

Froh Named art Loge,
But liar I call thee!

Donner Accursèd flame,
I will quench thy fire!

Loge From their shame to shelter,
Foolish folk flout me.

Donner threatens to strike Loge.

Wotan
Stepping between them. Forbear and let him alone!
Ye wot not Loge's wiles.

	His advice,
	Given slowly, gains
	Both in weight and in worth.
Fafner	Do not dally;
	Promptly pay!
Fasolt	Long waits our reward.
Wotan	
Turns sternly to Loge.	Speak up surly one!
	Fail me not!
	How far hast thou ranged and roamed?
Loge	Still with reproach
	Is Loge paid!
	Concerned but for thee,
	Thorough and swift,
	I searched and ransacked
	To the ends of the earth
	To find a ransom for Freia
	Fair to the giants and just.
	In vain the search,
	Convincing at last
	That the world contains
	Nothing so sweet
	That a man will take it instead
	Of woman's love and delight.
All seem surprised and taken aback.	
	Where life moves and has being,
	In water, earth and air
	I questioned,
	Asking of all things,
	Where weak still is strength,
	And germs only stirring,
	What men thought dear—
	And stronger deemed—
	Than woman's love and delight.
	But where life moves and has being
	My questions met
	But with laughter and scorn.

Varied gestures of amazement.

In water, earth and air
Woman and love
Will none forego.

One man, one only,
I met who, renouncing love,
Prized ruddy gold
Above any woman's grace.
The Rhine's pure-gleaming children
Told me of their sorrow.
The Nibelung,
Night-Alberich,
Wooed for the favour
Of the swimmers in vain,
And vengeance took,
Stealing the Rhinegold they guard.
He thinks it now
A thing beyond price,
Greater than woman's grace.
For their glittering toy
Thus torn from the deep
The sorrowful maids lamented.
They pray, Wotan,
Pleading to thee,
That thy wrath may fall on the robber
The gold too
They would have thee grant them
To guard in the water for ever.
Loge promised
The maidens to tell thee,
And, keeping faith, he has told.

Wotan

Dull thou must be
Or downright knavish!
In parlous plight myself,
What help have I for others?

Fasolt
Who has been listening attentively,
[to Fafner].

The Niblung has much annoyed us;
I greatly grudge him this Rhinegold;
But such his craft and cunning,
He has never been caught.

*The Rhine's pure-gleaming children
Told me of their sorrow.*

Fafner	Other malice Ponders the Niblung; Gains he might from gold Listen, Loge! Tell us the truth. What wondrous gift has the gold, That the dwarf desires it so?
Loge	A plaything, In the waves providing Children with laughter and sport, It gives, when to golden Ring it is rounded, Power and might unmatched; It wins its owner the world.
Wotan *Thoughtfully.*	Rumours I have heard Of the Rhinegold; Runes of riches Hide in its ruddy glow; Pelf and power Are by the ring bestowed.
Fricka *Softly to Loge.*	Could this gaud, This gleaming trinket Forged from the gold, Be worn by a woman too?
Loge	The wife who wore That glittering charm Never would lose Her husband's love— That charm which dwarfs are welding, Working in thrall to the ring.
Fricka *Coaxingly to Wotan.*	O could but my husband Come by the ring!
Wotan *As if falling more and more under the influence of a spell.*	Methinks it were wisdom, Won I the ring to my service. But say, Loge,

	How shall I learn
	To forge and fashion it true?
Loge	A magic rune
	Can round the golden ring.
	No one knows it,
	Yet plain the spell to him
	Who happy love forswears.
Wotan turns away in annoyance.	That suits thee not;
	Thou art too late too.
	Alberich did not delay;
	Fearless he mastered
	The potent spell,
Harshly.	And wrought aright was the ring.
Donner	We should all be
To Wotan.	Under the dwarf,
	Were not the ring from him wrested.
Wotan	The ring I must capture!
Froh	Lightly now,
	Without cursing love it were won.
Loge	Just so:
Harshly.	Without guile, as in children's games!
Wotan	Then tell us how.
Loge	By theft!
	What a thief stole
	Steal thou from the thief;
	How better could object be won?
	But with baleful arms
	Battles Alberich.
	Wary, wise
	Must be thy scheming,
	If the thief thou wouldst confound,
With warmth.	And restore the ruddy
	And golden toy,
	The Rhinegold, to the maidens.
	For this they pray and implore.

Wotan	The river-maidens?
	What profit were mine?
Fricka	Of that billow-born brood
	Bring me no tidings,
	For they have wooed
	To my woe
	Full many a man to their caves.

Wotan stands silent, struggling with himself. The other Gods gaze at him in mute suspense. Fafner, meanwhile, has been consulting aside with Fasolt.

Fafner	Worth far more than Freia
To Fasolt	Were the glittering gold.
	Eternal youth, too, were his
	Who could use the charm in its quest.

Fasolt's gestures indicate that he is being convinced against his will. Fafner and Fasolt approach Wotan again.

Fafner	Hear, Wotan,
	Our word while we wait;
	Freia we will restore you,
	And will take
	Paltrier payment:
	The Niblung's red-gleaming gold
	Will guerdon us giants rude.
Wotan	Ye must be mad!
	With what I possess not
	How can I, shameless ones, pay you?
Fafner	Hard labour
	Went to those walls;
	How easy
	With fraud-aided force
	(What our malice never achieved)
	The Niblung to break and bind!
Wotan	Why should I make
More quickly.	War on the Niblung?—
	Fight, your foe to confound?

>   Insolent
>   And greedily grasping
>   Dolts you grow through my debt!

Fasolt
Suddenly seizes Freia and drags her to one side with Fafner.
>   Maiden, come!
>   We claim thee ours!
>   As pledge thou shalt be held
>   Till the ransom is paid.

Freia   Woe's me! Woe's me! Woe!
Screaming.

Fafner
>   From your midst
>   We bear her forth!
>   Till evening—mark it well!—
>   As a pledge she is ours.
>   We will return then.
>   But when we come,
>   If the Rhinegold be not ready,
>   The Rhinegold bright and red—

Fasolt
>   The respite is ended,
>   Freia is forfeit
>   And bides among us for aye!

Freia
>   Sister! Brothers!
>   Save me! Help!

The giants hasten off, dragging Freia with them.

Froh   Up! Follow fast!

Donner   Fall now the heavens!
They look inquiringly at Wotan.

Freia   Save me! Help!
In the distance.

Fasolt suddenly seizes Freia and drags her to one side with Fafner.

Loge *Looking after the giants.*	Downward over stock and stone Striding they go; Through the ford across the Rhine Wade now the robbers. Sad at heart Hangs Freia, Thrown rudely over rough shoulders! Heia! hei! The louts, how they lumber along! Through the Rhine valley they reel. Not till Riesenheim's march Is reached will they rest!
He turns to the Gods.	
	How darkly Wotan doth dream! What ails the high, happy Gods?

A pale mist, gradually increasing in density, fills the stage. Seen through it the Gods look more and more wan and aged. All stand in dismay and apprehension regarding Wotan, whose eyes are fixed broodingly on the ground.

Loge	Does a mist mock me? Tricks me a dream? Dismayed and wan, How swiftly ye fade! Lo! the bloom forsakes your cheeks, And quenched is the light of your eyes! Courage, Froh! Day's but begun! From thy hand, Donner, The hammer is falling! And why frets Fricka? Sees she with sorrow That Wotan's hair, growing grey, Has made him gloomy and old?
Fricka	Woe's me! Woe's me! What does it mean?
Donner	My hand sinks down.
Froh	My heart stands still.

Loge

I have it: hear what ye lack!
Of Freia's fruit
Ye have not partaken to-day.
The golden apples
Within her garden
Restored you your strength and your youth,
Ate ye thereof each day.
The garden's guardian
In pledge has been given.
On the branches dries
And droops the fruit,
To drop soon and decay.
My loss is lighter,
For still did Freia,
Stingy to me,
Stint the delectable fruit.
Not half as godlike
Am I, ye high ones, as you!

Freely, but quickly and harshly.

But ye trusted solely
To the fruit that makes young,
As well both the giants wist.
Your life they played for,
Plotted to take;
Contrive so that they fail.
Lacking the apples,
Old and worn,
Grey and weary,
Wasting, the scoff of the world,
The Gods must pine and pass.

Fricka
Anxiously

Wotan, alas!
Unhappy man!
See what thy laughing
Lightness has brought us—
Scoff and scorn for all!

Wotan
Coming to a sudden resolve, starts up

Up, Loge,
And follow me!
To Nibelheim hastening downward,
I go in search of the gold.

The Gods grow wan and aged at the loss of Freia

Loge	The Rhine-daughters Thy aid invoked: Not vainly they hoped for thy help then?
Wotan *Angrily.*	Fool, be silent! Freia, the fair one— Freia's ransom we go for.
Loge	Where thou wouldst go Gladly I lead. Shall we dive Sheer through the depths of the Rhine?
Wotan	Not through the Rhine.
Loge	Then swift let us swing Through this smoky chasm. Together, come, creep we in!

He goes in front and vanishes at the side through a cleft, from which, immediately afterwards, sulphurous vapour streams forth.

Wotan	Ye others wait Till evening here; The golden ransom When got will again make us young.

He descends after Loge into the chasm. The sulphurous vapour which rises from it spreads over the whole stage and quickly fills it with thick clouds. Those who remain behind are soon hidden.

Donner	Fare thee well, Wotan!
Froh	Good luck! Good luck!
Fricka	O come back soon To thy sorrowing wife!

The sulphurous vapour darkens till it becomes a black cloud, which rises upwards from below. This then changes to a dark, rocky cavern which keeps rising, so that the stage seems to sink deeper and deeper into the earth.

THIRD SCENE

From various points in the distance ruddy lights gleam out. An increasing clamour, as of smiths at work, is heard on all sides. The clang of the anvils dies away. A vast subterranean chasm becomes visible which seems to open into narrow gorges on all sides. Alberich drags the screaming Mime out of a side cleft.

Alberich	Héhé! Héhé! Come here! Come here! Mischievous dwarf! Prettily pinched Promptly thou'lt be Hast thou not ready, Wrought to my wish, The dainty thing I desire!
Mime *Howling.*	Ohé! Ohé! Oh! Oh! Let me alone! It is forged; Heeding thy hest I laboured hard Till it was done! Take but thy nails from my ear!
Alberich	Then why this delay To show thy work?
Mime	I feared that something Might still be wanting.

Mime howling "Ohé! Ohé! Oh! Oh!"

Alberich What is there to finish?

Mime Here – and there –
Embarrassed.

Alberich How here and there?
Hand me the thing!

He tries to catch hold of his ear again. In his terror Mime drops a piece of metalwork which he has been clutching convulsively. Alberich picks it up hastily and examines it with care.

Rogue, observe!
See how all wrought is
Well finished and feat,
Done as desired!
The simpleton wants
Slyly to trick me
And keep by cunning
The wonderful work,
Though all his skill
Came alone from my craft.
Thou art discovered, thief.

He puts the Tarnhelm on his head.

The helmet fits the head;
But will the spell prosper too?

Very softly.

"Night and darkness,
Seen of none!"

He vanishes, and a pillar of cloud takes his place.

Brother, canst see me?

Mime Where art thou? I see no one.
Looks round in amaze.

Alberich Then feel me instead,
Invisible. Thou lazy scamp!
Take that for thy thievish thoughts!

Mime
Writhes under the lathes he receives, Ohé! Ohé!
the sound of which is heard without Oh! Oh! Oh!
the whip being seen.

Alberich
Invisible and laughing.

Ha! ha! ha!
Ha! ha! ha!
I thank thee, blockhead;
Thy work has stood the test.
Hoho! Hoho!
Nibelungs all
Bow now to Alberich!
For he is everywhere,
Waiting and watching;
Peace and rest
Are past for ever;
Ye must all serve him,
Though see him can none;
Where he cannot be spied
Look out for his coming;
None shall escape from his thraldom!

Harshly.

Hoho! hoho!
Hearken, he nears:
The Nibelung's lord!

The pillar of cloud disappears in the background. Alberich's scolding voice is heard more and more faintly. Mime lies huddled up in pain. Wotan and Loge come down through a cleft in the rock.

Loge

Nibelheim here.
Through pale mists gleaming,
How bright yonder fiery sparks glimmer!

Mime

Oh! Oh! Oh!

Wotan

I hear loud groans.
Who lies on the ground?

Mime
Writhes under the lashes he receives.

Loge
Bends over Mime.

Why all this whimpering noise?

Mime

Ohé! Ohé!
Oh! Oh!

Mime writhes under the lashes he receives

Loge	Hei, Mime! Merry dwarf!
	Who beats and bullies thee so?
Mime	Leave me in peace, pray.
Loge	So much is certain,
	And more still. Hark!
He raises him with difficulty	Help I promise thee, Mime!
Mime	What help for me?
	To do his bidding
	My brother can force me,
	For I am bound as his slave.
Loge	But, Mime, how has he
	Thus made thee his thrall?
Mime	By evil arts
	Fashioned Alberich
	A yellow ring,
	From the Rhinegold forged,
	At whose mighty magic
	Trembling we marvel;
	This spell puts in his power
	The Nibelung hosts of night.
	Happy we smiths
	Moulded and hammered,
	Making our women
	Trinkets to wear—
	Exquisite Nibelung toys—
	And lightly laughed at our toil.
	The rogue now compels us
	To creep into caverns,
	For him alone
	To labour unthanked.
	Through the golden ring
	His greed can divine
	Where untouched treasure
	In hidden gorge gleams.
	We still must keep spying,
	Peering and delving:

	Must melt the booty,
	Which, molten, we forge
	Without pause or peace,
	To heap up higher his hoard.
Loge	Just now, then, an idler
	Roused him to wrath?
Mime	Poor Mime, ah!
	My lot was the hardest.
	I had to work,
	Forging a helmet,
	With strict instructions
	How to contrive it;
	And well I marked
	The wondrous might
	Bestowed by the helm
	That from steel I wrought.
	Hence I had gladly
	Held it as mine,
	And, by its virtue
	Risen at last in revolt:
	Perchance, yes, perchance
	The master himself I had mastered,
	And, he in my power, had wrested
	The ring from him and used it
	That he might serve me, the free man,
Harshly	As now I must serve him, a slave!
Loge	And wherefore, wise one,
	Sped not the plan?
Mime	Ah! though the helm I fashioned,
	The magic that lurks therein
	I foolishly failed to divine.
	He who set the task
	And seized the fruits—
	From him I have learnt,
	Alas! but too late!
	All the helmet's cunning craft.
	From my sight he vanished,

Howling and sobbing *Rubs his back. Wotan and Loge laugh*	But, viciously lashing, Swung his arm through unseen. This, fool that I am, Was all my thanks!
Loge *To Wotan.*	Confess, our task Will call for skill.
Wotan	Yet the foe will yield, Use thou but fraud.
Mime *Observes the Gods more attentively*	Who are you, ye strangers That ask all these questions?
Loge	Friends to thee, Who from their straits Will free all the Nibelung folk.
Mime *Shrinking back in fear when he hears Alberich returning.*	Hark! Have a care! Alberich comes!

He runs to and fro in terror.

Wotan We'll wait for him here.

He sits down calmly on a stone. Alberich, who has taken the Tarnhelm from his head and hung it on his girdle, is brandishing his scourge and driving before him a band of Nibelungs from the gorges below. These are laden with gold and silver treasure, which, urged on by Alberich, they pile up so as to form a large heap.

Alberich Hither! Thither!
Héhé! Hoho!
Lazy herd!
Haste and heap
Higher the hoard.
Up with thee there!
On with thee here!
Indolent dolts,
Down with the treasure!
Need ye my urging?
Here with it all!

Alberich drives in a band of Nibelungs,
laden with gold and silver treasure

He suddenly perceives Wotan and Loge.	Hey! Who are they That thus intrude? Mime! Come here! Rascally rogue! Gossiping art With the pilgriming pair? Off, thou idler! Back to thy bellows and beating!
Lashing Mime, he chases him into the crowd of Nibelungs.	Hey! to your labour! Get ye all hence now! Swing ye down swift! From the virgin gorges Get me the gold! This whip will follow, Delve ye not fast! That labour ye shirk not Mime be surety, Or surely the lash Of my whip will find him; That where no one would guess I watch and I wander, None knows it better than he. Loitering still? Lingering there?
He pulls the ring from his finger, kisses it and stretches it out in menace.	Fear ye and tremble, O fallen host, And obey The ring's dread lord!

Howling and shrieking, the Nibelungs, among them Mime, scatter, and creep down into the clefts in all directions.

Alberich
Looks long and distrustfully at Wotan and Loge

What seek ye here?

Wotan

From Nibelheim's gloomy realm
Strange tidings have travelled up,
Tales of wonders
Worked here by Alberich;
And, greedy of marvels,
Hither came we as guests.

Alberich	By envy urged,
	Hither ye hie.
	Such doughty guests
	I do not mistake.
Loge	Since I am known,
	Ignorant elf,
	Say then, with growling
	Whom dost thou greet?
	In caverns cold
	Where once thou didst crouch,
	Who gave thee light
	And fire for thy comfort,
	Had Loge not smiled on thee?
	Or what hadst thou fashioned
	Had not I heated thy forge?
	I am thy kinsman
	And once was kind:
	Lukewarm, methinks, are thy thanks!
Alberich	On light-born elves
	Laughs now Loge,
	The crafty rogue:
	Art thou, false one, their friend
	As my friend thou wert once,
	Haha! I laugh!
	No harm from such need I fear.
Loge	No cause then for thy distrust.
Alberich	I can trust thy falsehood,
	Not thy good faith!
Taking up a defiant attitude	
	Yet I dare you all unflinching.
Loge	'Tis thy might
	That makes thee so bold;
	Grimly great
	Groweth thy power.

Alberich	Seest thou the hoard
	  Yonder heaped
	  High by my host?

Loge	A richer one never was seen.

Alberich	A wretched pile
	  Is this to-day, though.
	  Boldly mounting,
	  'Twill be bigger henceforward.

Wotan	But what is gained by the hoard
	  In joyless Nibelheim,
	  Where wealth finds nothing to buy?

Alberich	Treasure to gather
	  And treasure to garner—
	  Thereto Nibelheim serves.
	  But with the hoard
	  In the caverns upheaped
	  Wonders all wonder surpassing
	  Will I perform
	  And win the whole world and its fairness.

Wotan	But, my friend, how compass that goal?

Alberich	Ye who live above and breathe
	  The balmy, sweet airs,
	  Love and laugh:
	  A hand of gold
	  Ere long, O ye Gods, will have gripped you!
	  As I forswore love, even so
	  No one alive
	  But shall forswear it;
	  By golden songs wooed,
	  For gold alone will his greed be.
	  On hills of delight
	  Your home is, where gladness
	  Softly lulls;
	  The dark elves

	Ye despise, O deathless carousers!
	Beware!
	Beware!
	For first your men
	Shall bow to my might;
	Then your women fair
	Who my wooing spurned
	The dwarf will force to his will,
Laughing savagely	Though frowned on by love.
	Ha! ha! ha! ha!
	Mark ye my word?
	Beware!
	Beware of the hosts of the night,
	When rise shall the Nibelung hoard
	From silent depths to the day!
Wotan *Furiously.*	Avaunt, impious fool!
Alberich	What says he?
Loge *Stepping between them*	Cease from thy folly!
To Alberich	Who would gaze not in wonder,
	Beholding Alberich's work?
	If only thy skill can achieve
	Everything hope has promised,
	Almighty I needs must acclaim thee!
	For moon and stars
	And the sun in his glory,
	Forced to do thee obeisance,
	Even they must bow down.
	But what would seem of most moment
	Is that they who serve thee,
	The Nibelung hosts,
	Bow and bear no hate.
	When thy hand held forth a ring
	Thy folk were stricken with fear.
	But in thy sleep
	A thief might slip up
	And steal slyly the ring.
	Say, how wouldst thou save thyself
	then?

Alberich

Most shrewd to himself seems Loge;
Others always
Figure as fools.
If I had to ask for
Advice or aid
On bitter terms,
How happy the thief would be!
This helmet that hides
I schemed for myself,
And chose for its smith
Mime, finest of forgers.
I am now able
Swift to assume
Any form that I fancy,
Through the helm.
No one sees me,
Search as he will;
Though everywhere hidden,
I always am there.
So, fearing nothing,
Even from thee I am safe,
Most kind, careful of friends!

Loge

I have met
Full many a marvel,
But one so wondrous
Have never known.
Achievement so matchless
Scarce can I credit.
Were this possible, truly
Thy might indeed were eternal.

Alberich

Dost thou believe
I lie, as would Loge?

Loge

Till it is proved
I must suspect thy word.

Alberich

Puffed up with wisdom,
The fool will explode soon:
Of envy then die!

	Decide to what I shall change;
	In that form I shall stand.
Loge	Nay, choose for thyself,
	But strike me dumb with amaze.
Alberich	"Dragon dread,
Puts the Tarnhelm on his head	Wreathe thou and wriggle!"

He immediately disappears. An enormous serpent writhes on the floor in his place. It rears and threatens Wotan and Loge with its open jaws.

Loge *Pretends to be terrified*	Ohé!
Alberich *Laughing*	Ha! ha! ha! ha! ha! ha!
Loge	Ohé! Ohé!
	Horrible dragon,
	O swallow me not!
	Spare the life of poor Loge!
Wotan	Good, Alberich!
	Well done, rascal!
	How swiftly grew
	The dwarf to the dragon immense!

The dragon disappears and, in its stead, Alberich is again seen in his own shape.

Alberich	He he! Ye scoffers,
	Are ye convinced?
Loge	My trembling tells thee how truly.
In a trembling voice	A giant snake
	Thou wert in a trice.
	Having beheld,
	I just credit the wonder.
	Couldest thou turn
	To something quite tiny
	As well as bigger?
	Methinks that way were best
	For slyly slipping from foes;
	That, though, I fear were too hard!

Ohé! Ohé! Horrible dragon,
O swallow me not! Spare the life of poor Loge!

Alberich	For thee, yes;
	Thou art so dull!
	How small shall I be?
Loge	The most cramped of crannies must hold thee
	That hides the timorous toad.
Alberich	Nothing simpler!
	Look at me now!
	He puts the Tarnhelm on his head again.
	"Crooked toad,
	Creep and crawl there!"

He vanishes. The Gods see a toad on the rocks creeping towards them.

Loge *To Wotan*	Quick and catch it!
	Capture the toad!

Wotan sets his foot on the toad. Loge makes a dash at its head and holds the Tarnhelm in his hand.

Alberich

Is suddenly seen in his own shape writhing under Wotan's foot.
Ohé! I'm caught!
My curse upon them!

Loge	Hold him fast
	Till he is bound.

Loge binds his hands and feet with a rope.
Now swiftly up!
Then he is ours.

Both seize hold of the prisoner, who struggles violently, and drag him towards the shaft by which they descended. They disappear mounting upwards.

FOURTH SCENE

The scene has changed as before, only in reverse order. Open space on mountain heights. The prospect is veiled by pale mist as at the end of the second scene. Wotan and Loge climb up out of the cavern, bringing with them Alberich bound.

Loge	Here, kinsman,
	Thou canst sit down!
	Friend, look round thee;
	There lies the world
	That was thine for the winning, thou fool!
He dances round Alberich,	What corner, say,
snapping his fingers	Wilt give to me for my stall?
Alberich	Infamous robber!
	Thou knave! Thou rogue!
	Loosen the rope,
	Set me at large,
	Or dear for this outrage shalt answer!
Wotan	My captive art thou,
	Caught and in fetters.
	As thou hadst fain
	Subdued the world
	And all that the world containeth,
	Thou liest bound at my feet,
	And, coward, canst not deny it.
	A ransom alone
	Shall loose thee from bondage.
Alberich	Ah, the dolt,
	The dreamer I was,
	To trust blindly
	The treacherous thief!
	Fearful revenge
	Shall follow this wrong!

Loge	Vain talk this of vengeance
	Before thy freedom is won.
	To a man in bonds
	No free man expiates outrage.
	If vengeance thou dreamest,
	Dream of the ransom
	First without further delay!

He shows him the kind of ransom by snapping his fingers.

Alberich	Declare then your demands.
Wotan	The hoard and thy gleaming gold.
Alberich	Pack of unscrupulous thieves!
Aside.	If I only can keep the ring,
	The hoard I can lightly let go,
	For anew I could win it
	And add to its worth
	By the powerful spell of the ring.
	If as warning it serves
	To make me more wise,
	The warning will not have been lost,
	Even though lost may be the gold.
Wotan	Wilt yield up the hoard?
Alberich	Loosen my hand
	To summon it here.

Loge frees his right hand.

Alberich
Touches the ring with his lips and secretly murmurs the command.
                Behold the Nibelungs
                Hither are called;
                I can hear them coming,
                Bid by their lord,
                With the hoard from the depths to the day.
                Now loosen these burdensome bonds.

Wotan Nay, first in full thou must pay.

The Nibelungs come up out of the cleft laden with the objects of which the hoard is composed.

Alberich O bitter disgrace
That my shrinking bondsmen
Should see me captive and bound!

To the Nibelungs.

Lay it down there,
As ye are bid!
In a heap
Pile up the hoard.
Must I aid, idlers?
No spying at me!
Haste there! Haste!
Then get ye gone quickly.
Hence to your work.
Home to your gorges!
Let the sluggards beware,
For I follow hard at your heels!

He kisses the ring and holds it out with an air of command. As struck with a blow, the Nibelungs press terrified and cowering towards the cleft, down which they hastily disappear.

Alberich The price is paid;
Let me depart!
And that helm of mine
Which Loge still holds,
That also pray give me again!

Loge The plunder must pay for the pardon.
Throwing the Tarnhelm on to the heap.

Alberich Accursed thief!
But patience! Calm!
He who moulded the one
Makes me another;
Still mine is the might
That Mime obeys.
Loath indeed

	Am I to leave My cunning defence to the foe! Nothing Alberich Owns at all now; Unbind, ye tyrants, his bonds!
Loge *To Wotan.*	Ought I to free him? Art thou content?
Wotan	A golden ring Girdles thy finger: Hearest, elf? That also belongs to the hoard.
Alberich *Horrified.*	The ring?
Wotan	The ring must also Go to the ransom.
Alberich *Trembling.*	My life—but the ring: not that!
Wotan *With greater violence.*	The ring I covet; For thy life I care not at all.
Alberich	But if my life I ransom The ring I must also rescue Hand and head, Eye and ear Are not mine more truly Than mine is the ruddy ring!
Wotan	The ring thou claimest as thine? Impudent elf, thou art raving. Tell the truth; Whence was gotten the gold To fashion the glittering gaud? How could that be

Thine which reft was,
Thou rogue, from watery deeps?
To the Rhine's fair daughters
Down and inquire
If the gold
Was as gift to thee given
That thou didst thieve for the ring!

Alberich

Vile double-dealing!
Shameless deceit!
Wouldst thou, robber,
Reproach in me
The sin so sweet to thyself?
How fain thou hadst
Bereft the Rhine of its gold,
If it had been
As easy to forge as to steal!
How well for thee,
Thou unctuous knave,
That the Nibelung, stung
By shameful defeat,
And by fury driven,
Was fired into winning the spell
That now alluringly smiles!
Shall I, bliss debarred,
Anguish-burdened
Because of the
Curse-laden deed,
My ring as a toy
Grant to princes for pleasure,
My ban bringing blessing to thee?
Have a care,
Arrogant God!
My sin was one
Concerning myself alone:
But against all that was,
Is and shall be
Thou wouldst wantonly sin,
Eternal one, taking the ring.

Wotan

Yield the ring!
Thy foolish talk
Gives no title to that.

He seizes Alberich and draws the ring from his finger by force.

Alberich
With a frightful cry.

Woe! Defeated! Undone!
Of wretches the wretchedest slave!

Wotan
Contemplating the ring.

I own what makes me supreme,
The mightiest lord of all lords!

He puts on the ring.

Loge *To Wotan.*

Shall he go free?

Wotan

Loose his bonds.

Loge
Sets Alberich quite free.

Slip away home,
For no fetter binds thee!
Fare forth, thou art free!

Alberich
Raising himself with furious laughter

Am I now free,
Free in truth?
My freedom's first
Greeting take, for it is thine!
As a curse gave me the ring,
My curse go with the ring!
As its gold
Gave measureless might,
May now its magic
Deal death evermore!
No man shall gain
Gladness therefrom;
May ill-fortune befall him
On whom it shines.
Fretted by care
Be he who shall hold it,
And he who doth not,
By envy be gnawed!
All shall covet

                                          And crave its wealth,
                                          Yet none shall it profit
                                          Or pay when won.
                                          Those who guard it nothing shall gain,
                                          Yet shall murder go where they go.
                                          The coward, death-doomed,
                                          By fetters of fear shall be bound;
                                          His whole life long
                                          He shall languish to death—
                                          The ring's proud lord
                                          And its poorest slave—
                                          Till again I have
                                          In my hand the gold I was robbed of.
                                          So blesses
                                          The Nibelung
                                          The ring in bitter despair!
                                          Hold fast to it!
Laughing.   Keep it with care;
Grimly.   From my curse none shall escape!

He vanishes quickly through the cleft. The thick mist in the foreground gradually clears away.

Loge   Hadst thou ears
                                          For his fond farewell?

Wotan *Left in contemplation of the ring.*   Grudge him not vent to his spleen!
It keeps growing lighter.

Loge *Looking to the right.*   Fasolt and Fafner
                                          Come from afar
                                          Bringing Freia again.
Through the vanishing mist Donner, Froh, and Fricka appear,
and hasten towards the foreground.

Froh   The giants return.

Donner   Be greeted, brother!

Fricka   Dost bring joyful tidings?
Anxiously to Wotan.

Loge
Pointing to the hoard.

Donner

Froh

By fraud and by force
We have prevailed:
There Freia's ransom lies.
From the giant's grasp
Freed comes the fair one.

How sweetly the air
Fans us again!
Balmy delights
Steal soft through each sense!
Sad, forlorn had our lot been,
For ever severed from her
Who gives us youth everlasting,
And bliss triumphant o'er pain.

Fasolt and Fafner enter, leading Freia between them. Fricka hastens joyfully towards her sister. The foreground has become quite bright again, the light restoring to the aspect of the Gods its original freshnesh. The background, however, is still veiled by the mist so that the distant castle remains invisible.

Fricka

Sweetest of sisters!
Lovely delight!
Once more for mine have I won thee!

Fasolt
Keeping her off

Hold! Touch her not yet!
Freia still is ours.
On Riesenheim's
Rampart of rock
Resting we stayed.
The pledge we held
In our hands we used
Loyally.
With deep regret,
I bring her back now
In case ye brothers
Can ransom her.

Wotan

Prepared lies the ransom;
Mete out the gold,
Giving generous measure.

Fasolt	In truth it grieves me Greatly the woman to lose; And that my heart may forget her Ye must heap the hoard, Pile it so high That it shall hide The blossom-sweet maid from mine eyes!
Wotan	Be Freia's form The gauge of the gold.

Freia is placed in the middle by the two giants, who then stick their staves into the ground in front of her so that her height and breadth is indicated.

Fafner	Our staves give the measure Of Freia's form; Thus high now heap ye the hoard.
Wotan	On with the work: Irksome I find it!
Loge	Help me, Froh!
Froh	I will end Freia's dishonour.

Loge and Froh heap up the treasure hastily between the staves.

Fafner	Let the pile Less loosely be built; Firm and close Pack ye the gauge!

He presses down the treasure with rude strength; he bends down to look for gaps.

	I still can see through; Come, fill up the crannies!
Loge	Hands off, rude fellow! Touch nothing here!
Fafner	Come here! This gap must be closed!

Wotan
Turning away angrily.

Deep in my breast
Burns the disgrace!

Fricka

See how in shame
Beautiful Freia stands;
For release she asks,
Dumb, with sorrowful eyes.
Heartless man!
The lovely one owes this to thee!

Fafner

Still more! Pile on still more.

Donner

My patience fails;
Mad is the wrath
Roused by this insolent rogue!
Come hither, hound!
Measure must thou?
Thy strength then measure with mine!

Fafner

Softly, Donner!
Roar where it serves;
Thy roar is impotent here.

Donner
Lunging out at him.

It will crush thee to thy cost, rogue.

Wotan

Calm thyself!
Methinks that Freia is hid.

Loge

The hoard is spent.

Fafner

Still shines to me Holda's hair.

Measures the hoard carefully with his eye, and looks to see if there are any crevices.

Yonder thing, too,
Throw on the hoard!

Loge

Even the helm?

Fafner	Make haste!
	Here with it!
Wotan	Let it go also!
Loge	At last we have finished.
Throws the Tarnhelm on the heap	Have ye enough now?
Fasolt	Freia, the fair,
	Is hidden for aye!
	The price has been paid.
	Ah, have I lost her?

He goes up to the hoard and peers through it.

	Sadly shine
	Her eyes on me still,
	Like stars they beam
	Softly on me;
	Still through this chink
	I look on their light.
Beside himself.	While her sweet eyes I behold thus,
	From the woman how can I part?
Fafner	Hey! Come hither,
	And stop me this cranny!
Loge	Greedy grumblers!
	Can ye not see
	The gold is all gone?
Fafner	Not the whole, friend!
	On Wotan's finger
	Shines a golden ring still;
	Give that to close up the crevice!
Wotan	What! Give my ring?
Loge	Be ye counselled!
	The Rhine-Maidens
	Must have the gold;
	Wotan will give them what theirs is.

"Hey! Come hither,
And stop me this cranny!"

Wotan	What nonsense is this?
	The ring I won so hardly,
	Undismayed I hold and will keep.
Loge	Broken then
	Must be the promise
	I gave the maidens who grieved.
Wotan	By thy promise I am not bound;
	As booty mine is the ring.
Fafner	Not so. The ring
	Must go with the ransom.
Wotan	Boldly ask what ye will:
	It shall be granted;
	But not for all
	The world would I give you the ring.
Fasolt	All is off!
Furious, pulls Freia from	The bargain stands:
behind the hoard.	Fair Freia ours is for ever!
Freia	Help me! Help me!
Fricka	Heartless God,
	Grant it! Give way!
Froh	Keep not the gold back!
Donner	Give them the ring too!
Wotan	Let me alone!
	I hold to the ring.

Fafner stops Fasolt as he is hastening off. All stand dismayed; Wotan turns from them in anger. The stage has grown dark again. From a cleft in the rock on one side issues a bluish flame in which Erda suddenly becomes visible, rising so that her upper half is seen.

Erda
Stretching out a warning hand towards Wotan.

Yield it, Wotan! Yield it!
Flee the ring's dread curse!
Awful
And utter disaster
It will doom thee to.

Wotan

What woman woe thus foretells?

Erda

All things that were I know,
And things that are;
All things that shall be
I foresee.
The endless world's
Ur-Wala,
Erda, bids thee beware.
Ere the earth was,
Of my womb born
Were daughters three;
And my knowledge
Nightly the Norns tell to Wotan.
Now summoned by
Danger most dire,
I myself come.
Hearken! Hearken! Hearken!
All things will end shortly;
And for the Gods
Dark days are dawning!
Be counselled; keep not the ring!

Erda sinks slowly as far as the breast, while the bluish light grows fainter.

Wotan

A mystic might
Rang in thy words.
Tarry, and tell me further.

Erda
Disappearing.

Thou hast been warned;
Enough dost know;
Weigh my words with fear!

She vanishes completely.

Erda bids thee Beware!

Wotan	If thus doomed to foreboding—
	I must detain thee
	Till all is answered!

Wotan is about to follow Erda in order to detain her. Froh and Fricka throw themselves in his way and prevent him.

Fricka	What meanest thou, madman?
Froh	Go not, Wotan!
	Fear thou the warner,
	Heed her words well!

Wotan gazes thoughtfully before him

Donner	Hark, ye giants!
Turning to the giants with a	Come back and wait still!
resolute air.	The gold we give you also.
Fricka	Ah, dare I hope it?
	Deem ye Holda
	Worthy of such a price?

All look at Wotan in suspense; he, rousing himself from deep thought, grasps his spear and swings it in token of having come to a bold decision.

Wotan	To me, Freia,
	For thou art free!
	Bought back for aye,
	Youth everlasting, return!
	Here, giants, take ye the ring!

He throws the ring on the hoard. The giants release Freia; she hastens joyfully to the Gods, who caress her in turns for a space, with every manifestation of delight.

Fasolt	Hold there, greedy one!
To Fafner.	Grant me my portion!
	Honest division
	Best for both is.
Fafner	More on the maid than the gold
	Thou wert set, love-sick fool,
	And much against

	Thy will the exchange was.
	Sharing not, Freia
	Thou wouldst have wooed for thy bride;
	Sharing the gold,
	It is but just
	That the most of it should be mine.
Fasolt	Infamous thief!
	Taunts? And to me!
To the Gods.	Come judge ye between us;
	Halve ye the hoard
	As seems to you just!

Wotan turns away in contempt

Loge	Let him have the treasure;
	Hold to what matters: the ring!

Fasolt
Falls upon Fafner, who has meanwhile been steadily packing up the treasure.

	Back, brazen rascal!
	Mine is the ring.
	I lost for it Freia's smile.
He snatches haply at the ring.	Off with thy hands!
	The ring is mine.

There is a struggle. Fasolt tears the ring from Fafner.

Fasolt	I hold it. It is mine now!
Fafner	Hold fast, lest it should fall!

Lunging out with his stave, he fells Fasolt to the ground with one blow; from the dying man he then hastily tears the ring.

	Now feast upon Freia's smile:
	No more shalt thou touch the ring!

He puts the ring into the sack and tranquilly continues to pack up the rest of the hoard. All the Gods stand horrified. A solemn silence.

Wotan	Dread indeed
	I find is the curse's might.

Fafner kills Fasolt

Loge

Unmatched, Wotan,
Surely thy luck is!
Great thy gain was
In getting the ring;
But the gain of its loss
Is gain greater still:
There thy foemen, see,
Slaughter thy foes
For the gold thou hast let go.

Wotan

Dark forebodings oppress me!
Care and fear
Fetter my soul;
Erda must teach me,
Tell how to end them:
To her I must descend.

Fricka
Caressing and coaxing him.

Why linger, Wotan?
Beckon they not,
The stately walls,
Waiting to offer
Welcome kind to their lord?

Wotan
Gloomily.

With wage accurst
Paid was their cost.

Donner *Pointing to the background, which is still enveloped in mist.*

Heavily mists
Hang in the air;
Gloomy, wearisome
Is their weight!
The wan-visaged clouds
Charged with their storms I will gather,
And sweep the blue heavens clean.

Donner mounts a high rock on the edge of the precipice, and swings his hammer; during what follows the mists gather round him.

Hey da! Hey da! Hey do!
To me, O ye mists!
Ye vapours, to me!
Donner, your lord,
Summons his hosts!

Donner, your lord, summons his hosts!

He swings his hammer.　　　　　　To my hammer's swing
　　　　　　　　　　　　　　　　Hitherward sweep
　　　　　　　　　　　　　　　　Vapours and fogs!
　　　　　　　　　　　　　　　　Hovering mists!
　　　　　　　　　　　　　　　　Donner, your lord, summons his hosts!
　　　　　　　　　　　　　　　　Hey da! Hey da! Hey do!

Donner disappears completely in a thunder-cloud which has been growing darker and denser. The stroke of his hammer is heard falling heavily on the rock. A vivid flash of lightning comes from the cloud, followed by a loud clap of thunder. Froh has also disappeared in the cloud.

Donner　　　　　　　　　　　Brother, to me!
Invisible.　　　　　　　　　　　Show them the way by the bridge!

Suddenly the clouds roll away. Donner and Froh become visible. A rainbow of dazzling radiance stretches from their feet across the valley to the castle, which is gleaming in the light of the setting sun.

With outstretched hand, Froh indicates to the Gods that the bridge is the way across the valley.

Froh　　　　　　　　　　　　Lo, light, yet securely,
　　　　　　　　　　　　　　　　Leads the bridge to your halls.
　　　　　　　　　　　　　　　　Undaunted tread;
　　　　　　　　　　　　　　　　Without danger the road!

Wotan and the other Gods stand speechless, lost in contemplation of the glorious sight.

Wotan　　　　　　　　　　　Smiling at eve
　　　　　　　　　　　　　　　　The sun's eye sparkles;
　　　　　　　　　　　　　　　　The castle ablaze
　　　　　　　　　　　　　　　　Gleams fair in its glow.
　　　　　　　　　　　　　　　　In the light of morning
　　　　　　　　　　　　　　　　Glittering proudly,
　　　　　　　　　　　　　　　　It stood masterless,
　　　　　　　　　　　　　　　　Stately, tempting its lord.
　　　　　　　　　　　　　　　　From dawn until sundown
　　　　　　　　　　　　　　　　No little toil
　　　　　　　　　　　　　　　　And fear have gone to the winning!
　　　　　　　　　　　　　　　　From envious night,
　　　　　　　　　　　　　　　　That now draws nigh
　　　　　　　　　　　　　　　　Shelter it offers us.
Very firmly, as if struck by a great thought.　So greet I my home,

He turns solemnly to Fricka.	Safe from dismay and dread. Follow me, wife! In Valhall sojourn with me.
Fricka	What means the name Valhall? I never seem to have heard it.
Wotan	That which, conquering fear, My fortitude brought Triumphant to birth— Let that explain the word!

He takes Fricka's hand and walks slowly with her towards the bridge. Froh, Freia, and Donner follow.

Loge *Remaining in the foreground and looking after the Gods.*

> They are hasting on to their end,
> They who dream they are strong and enduring.
> I almost blush
> To be of their number;
> A fancy allures me
> And wakes in me longing
> Flaming fire to become:
> To waste and burn them
> Who tamed me of old,
> Rather than perish,
> Blind with the blind—
> Yes, even if godlike the Gods were—
> More wise were it, perhaps!
> I must consider:
> The outcome who knows!

With a show of carelessness he goes to the Gods.

The Three Rhine-Maidens *From the valley. Invisible.*	Rhinegold! Rhinegold! Rhinegold pure! How radiant and clear Once thou didst shine on us! For thy lost glory We are grieving.

"The Rhine's fair children,
Bewailing their lost gold, weep"

	Give us the gold!
	Give us the gold!
	O give us the Rhinegold again!

Wotan *About to set his foot on the bridge, pauses and turns round.*

What wailing sound do I hear?

Loge
Looks down into the valley.

The Rhine's fair children,
Bewailing their lost gold, weep.

Wotan

Accursèd nixies!
Bid them tease us no more!

Loge
Calling down towards the valley.

Ye in the water,
Why wail ye to us?
List to Wotan's decree.
Ye have seen
The last of the gold;
In the Gods' increase of splendour
Bask and sun yourselves now.

The Gods laugh and cross the bridge during what follows.

The Three Rhine-Maidens

Rhinegold!
Rhinegold!
Rhinegold pure!
Oh, if in the waves
There but shone still our treasure pure!
Down in the deeps
Can faith be found only:
Mean and false
Are all who revel above!

As the Gods cross the bridge to the castle the curtain falls.

THE VALKYRIE

CHARACTERS
WOTAN HUNDING
FRICKA SIEGMUND
　　　　SIEGLINDE
BRÜNNHILDE, Valkyrie
EIGHT OTHER VALKYRIES:
Gerhilde, Ortlinde, Waltraute,
Schwertleite, Helmwige, Siegrune,
　　　Grimgerde, Rossweisse

SCENES OF ACTION
ACT I. THE INTERIOR OF HUNDING'S DWELLING
ACT II. A WILD ROCKY MOUNTAIN
ACT III. ON THE TOP OF A ROCKY MOUNTAIN
　　　　　　　　　(BRÜNNHILDE'S ROCK)

THE FIRST ACT

The interior of a dwelling-place built of wood, with the stem of a mighty ash-tree as its centre; to the right, in the foreground, is the hearth, and behind this the storeroom. At the back is the large entrance door; to the left, far back, steps lead up to an inner chamber; on the same side, nearer the front, stands a table with a broad bench behind it, fixed to the wall, and with stools in front. The stage remains empty for a space. Outside a storm is just subsiding. Siegmund opens the entrance door from without, and enters. With his hand on the latch he surveys the room. He seems overwhelmed with fatigue; his dress and appearance indicate that he is in flight. He shuts the door behind him when he sees nobody, walks to the hearth with the final effort of an utterly exhausted man, and throws himself down on a bearskin rug.

    Siegmund   I rest on this hearth,
                                        Heedless who owns it.

He sinks back and remains stretched out motionless. Sieglinde enters from the inner chamber; she thinks her husband has returned. Her grave look changes to one of surprise when she sees the stranger stretched out on the hearth.

    Sieglinde   A stranger here!
Still at the back.   He must be questioned.
                                        What man came in
Coming nearer.   And lies on the hearth?
As Siegmund does not move, she draws nearer still and looks at him.
                                        Way-worn, weary
                                        He seems and spent.
                                        Faints he from weariness?
She bends over him, and listens   Can he be sick?
                                        He breathes still, his eyelids
                                        Are sealed but in slumber.
                                        Worthy, valiant his mien,
                                        Though so worn he rests.

Siegmund
Suddenly raising his head   A drink! A drink!

Sieglinde   I go to fetch it.
She takes a drinking-horn and hurries out.
She returns with it full, and offers it.   Lo, the water
Thy thirsting lips longed for:
Water brought at thy wish!

Siegmund drinks, and hands her back the horn. As he signifies his thanks with a movement of the head, he gazes at her with growing interest.

Siegmund   Welcome the water!
Quenched is my thirst.
My weary load
Lighter it makes;
New courage it gives;
Mine eyes that slept
Re-open glad on the world.
Who soothes and comforts me so?

Sieglinde   This house and this wife
Belong to Hunding.
Stay thou here as his guest;
Tarry till he comes home.

Siegmund   Shelter he surely
Will grant a worn,
Wounded, weaponless stranger.

Sieglinde   Quick, show me! Where are thy wounds?
With anxious haste.

Siegmund
Shakes himself and springs up briskly   My wounds are slight,
to a sitting posture.   Scarce worthy remark;
My limbs are well knit still,
Whole and unharmed.
If my spear and shield had but been
Half so strong as my arm is,
I had vanquished the foe;
But in splinters were spear and shield.

The horde of foemen
Harassed me sore;
Through storm and strife
Spent was my force;
But, faster than I from foemen,
All my faintness has fled;
Darkness fell deep on my lids,
But now the sun again laughs.

Sieglinde
Goes to the storeroom, fills a horn with mead, and proffers it to Siegmund with friendly eagerness.

This healing and honeyed
Draught of mead
Deign to accept from me.

Siegmund

Set it first to thy lips.

Sieglinde sips from the horn and hands it back to him. Siegmund takes a long draught, regarding Sieglinde with increasing warmth. Still gazing, he takes the horn from his lips and lets it sink slowly, while his features express strong emotion. He sighs deeply, and lowers his gaze gloomily to the ground.

Siegmund
In a trembling voice.

Thou hast tended an ill-fated one!
May all evil
Be turned from thee!

He starts up quickly, and goes towards the the back.

I have been solaced
By sweet repose:
Onward now I must press.

Sieglinde
Turning round quickly.

Who pursues thee so close at thy heels?

Siegmund
Stops.

Bad luck pursues me,
Everywhere follows;
And where I linger
Trouble still finds me:
Be thou preserved from its touch!
I must not gaze but go.

He strides hastily to the door and lifts the latch.

Sieglinde
Forgetting herself calls impetuously after him.

Then tarry here!
Misfortune thou canst not bring
To those who abide with it!

"This healing and honeyed draught of mead
Deign to accept from me"

Siegmund
Deeply moved, remains standing; he looks searchingly at Sieglinde, who, ashamed and sad, lowers her eyes.
Returning, he leans against the hearth, his gaze fixed on Sieglinde. She continues silently embarrassed.

Wehwalt named I myself:

Hunding here will I wait for.

Sieglinde starts, listens and hears Hunding outside leading his horse to the stable. She hurries to the door and opens it. Hunding, armed with shield and spear, enters, but, perceiving Siegmund, pauses on the threshold. Hunding turns with a look of stern inquiry to Sieglinde.

Sieglinde
In answer to Hunding's look.

On the hearth
Fainting I found
One whom need drove here.

Hunding

Hast succoured him?

Sieglinde

I gave him, as a guest,
Welcome and a drink.

Siegmund
Regarding Hunding firmly and calmly.

Drink she gave,
Shelter too:
Wouldst therefore chide the woman?

Hunding
To Sieglinde, as he takes off his armour and hands it to her.

Sacred is my hearth:
Sacred hold thou my house.
Set the meal for us men!

Sieglinde hangs up the arms on the stem of the ash-tree, fetches food and drink from the store-room and sets supper on the table. Involuntarily she turns her gaze on Siegmund again.

Hunding
Examining Siegmund's features keenly and with amaze, compares them with Sieglinde's. Aside.

How like to the woman!
In his eye as well
Gleams the guile of the serpent.

He conceals his surprise, and turns with apparent unconcern to Siegmund.

Far, I trow,
Must thou have fared;

	The man who rests here Rode no horse: What toilsome journey Made thee so tired?
Siegmund	Through wood and meadow, Thicket and moor, Chased by the storm And peril sore, I ran by I know not what road. I know as little What goal it led to, And I would gladly be told.
Hunding *At table, inviting Siegmund* *to be seated.*	'Tis Hunding owns The roof and room Which have harboured thee. If to the westward Thou wert to wend, In homesteads rich Thou wouldst find kinsmen Who guard the honour of Hunding. May I ask of my guest In return to tell me his name?

Siegmund, who has taken his seat at the table, looks thoughtfully before him. Sieglinde, who has placed herself beside Hunding and opposite Siegmund, gazes at him with evident sympathy and suspense.

Hunding *Watching them both.*	If thou wilt not Trust it to me, To this woman tell thy secret: See, how eagerly she asks!
Sieglinde *Unembarrassed and interested.*	Gladly I'd know Who thou art.
Siegmund *Looks up and, gazing into her* *eyes, begins gravely.*	Not for me the name Friedmund; Frohwalt fain were I called, But forced was I to be Wehwalt.

Hunding discovers the likeness between Siegmund and Sieglinde

Wölfe they called my father;
And I am one of twins:
With a sister twin I was born.
Soon lost were
Both mother and maid;
I hardly knew
Her who gave me my life,
Nor her with whom I was born.
Warlike and strong was Wölfe,
And never wanting for foes.
A-hunting oft
Went the son with the father.
One day we returned
Outworn with the chase
And found the wolf's nest robbed.
The brave abode
To ashes was burnt,
Consumed to dust
The flourishing oak,
And dead was the mother,
Dauntless but slain.
No trace of the sister
Was ever found:
The Neidungs' heartless horde
Had dealt us this bitter blow.
My father fled,
An outlaw with me;
And the youth
Lived wild in the forest
With Wölfe for many years.
Sore beset and harried were they,
But boldly battled the pair of wolves.

Turning to Hunding. A Wölfing tells thee the tale,
And a well-known Wölfing, I trow.

Hunding

Wondrous and wild the story
Told by thee, valiant guest:
Wehwalt—the Wölfing!
I think that dark rumours anent
This doughty pair have reached me,
Though unknown Wölfe
And Wölfing too.

Sieglinde	But tell me further, stranger:
	Where dwells thy father now?
Siegmund	The Neidungs, starting anew,
	Hounded and hunted us down;
	But slain by the wolves
	Fell many a hunter;
	They fled through the wood,
	Chased by the game:
	Like chaff we scattered the foe.
	But trace of my father I lost;
	Still his trail grew fainter
	The longer I followed;
	In the wood a wolf-skin
	Was all I found;
	There empty it lay:
	My father I had lost.—
	In the woods I could not stay;
	My heart longed for men and for women.—
	By all I met,
	No matter where,
	If friend I sought,
	Or woman wooed,
	Still I was branded an outlaw;
	Ill-luck clung to me;
	Whatever I did right,
	Others counted it wrong;
	What seemed evil to me
	Won from others applause.
	Grim feuds arose
	Wherever I went;
	Wrath met me
	At every turn;
	Longing for gladness,
	Woe was my lot:
He looks at Sieglinde and	I called myself Wehwalt therefore,
marks her sympathetic gaze.	For woe was all that was mine.
Hunding	Thou wert shown no grace by the Norns
	That cast thy grievous lot;
	No one greets thee as guest
	With gladness in his home.

Sieglinde

Only cowards would fear
A weaponless, lonely man!—
Tell us, O guest,
How in the strife
At last thy weapon was lost!

Siegmund

A sorrowful child
Cried for my help;
Her kinsmen wanted
To wed the maiden
To one whom her heart did not choose.
To her defence
Gladly I hied;
The heartless horde
Met me in fight:
Before me foemen fell.
Fordone and dead lay the brothers.
The slain were embraced by the maid,
Her wrongs forgotten in grief.
She wept wild streams of woe,
And bathed the dead with her tears;
For the loss of her brothers slain
Lamented the ill-fated bride.
Then the dead men's kinsmen
Came like a storm,
Vowing vengeance,
Frantic to fall on me;
Foemen on all sides
Rose and assailed me.
But from the spot
Moved not the maid;
My shield and spear
Sheltered her long,
Till spear and shield
Were hewn from my hand.
Standing weaponless, wounded,
I beheld the maid die:
I fled from the furious host—

To Sieglinde with a look of fervent sorrow.

She lay lifeless on the dead.
The reason now I have told
Why none may know me as Friedmund.

He rises and walks to the hearth. Pale, deeply moved, Sieglinde looks on the ground.

Hunding *Rises.*	I know a wild-blooded breed; What others revere It flouts unawed: All hate it, and I with the rest. When forth in haste I was summoned, Vengeance to seek For my kinsmen's blood, I came too late, And now return home To find the impious wretch In haven under my roof.— My house holds thee, Wölfing, to-day; For the night thou art my guest. But wield to-morrow Thy trustiest weapon. I choose the day for the fight: Thy life shall pay for the dead.

To Sieglinde, who steps between the two men with anxious gestures; harshly.

Forth from the hall!
Linger not here!
Prepare my draught for the night,
And wait until I come.

Sieglinde stands for a while undecided and thoughtful. Slowly and with hesitating steps she goes towards the store-room, There she pauses again, lost in thought, her face half averted. With quiet resolution she opens the cupboard, fills a drinking-horn, and shakes spices into it out of a box. She then turns her eyes on Siegmund, in order to meet his gaze, which he never removes from her. She perceives that Hunding is watching, and proceeds immediately to the bed-chamber. On the steps she turns once more, looks yearningly at Siegmund, and indicates with her eyes, persistently and with speaking plainness, a particular spot in the stem of the ash-tree. Hunding starts, and drives her off with a violent gesture. With a last look at Siegmund, she disappears into the bed-chamber, and shuts the door behind her.

Hunding *Taking his weapons from the tree-stem.*	With weapons man should be armed. We meet to-morrow then Wölfing. My word thou hast heard; Ward thyself well!

He goes into the bed-chamber. The shooting of the bolt is heard from within.

Sieglinde prepares Hunding's draught for the night

Siegmund alone. It has grown quite dark. All the light in the hall comes from a dull fire on the hearth. Siegmund sinks down on to a couch beside the fire and broods for some time silently in great agitation.

Siegmund　　My father said when most wanted
　　　　　　A sword I should find and wield.
　　　　　　Swordless I entered
　　　　　　My foeman's house,
　　　　　　As a hostage here
　　　　　　I remain.
　　　　　　I saw a fair
　　　　　　Woman and sweet,
　　　　　　And bliss and dread
　　　　　　Consume my heart.
　　　　　　The woman for whom I long—
　　　　　　She whose charm both wounds and delights—
　　　　　　In thrall is held by the man
　　　　　　Who mocks a weaponless foe.
　　　　　　Wälse! Wälse!
　　　　　　Where is thy sword?—
　　　　　　The trusty sword
　　　　　　To be swung in battle,
　　　　　　When from my bosom should burst
　　　　　　The fury that fills my heart?

The fire collapses. From the flame which leaps up a bright light falls on the spot in the ash-tree's stem indicated by Sieglinde's look, and on which the hilt of a sword is now plainly visible.

　　　　　　What can that be
　　　　　　That shines so bright?
　　　　　　What a ray streams
　　　　　　From the ash-tree's stem!
　　　　　　My eyes that saw not
　　　　　　See the bright flash;
　　　　　　Gay as laughter it gleams.
　　　　　　How the radiant light
　　　　　　Illumes my heart!
　　　　　　Is it the look
　　　　　　That lingered behind,
　　　　　　Yonder clinging,
　　　　　　When forth from the hall
　　　　　　The lovely woman went?

From this point the fire gradually goes out.
>   Darkly the shadows
>   Covered my eyes,
>   Till her shining glance
>   Over me gleamed,
>   Bringing me warmth and day.
>   Gay and splendid
>   The sun appeared,
>   And blissfully circled
>   With glory my head—
>   Till by the hills it was hid.

The fire flickers up faintly again.
>   But once more, ere it set,
>   Bright it shone upon me,
>   And the ancient ash-tree's stem
>   Was lit by its golden glow.
>   The splendour passes,
>   The light grows dim,
>   Shadowy darkness
>   Falls and enshrouds me;
>   Deep in my bosom's fastness
>   Glimmers still faintly the flame!

The fire goes out altogether. Total darkness. The door of the bed-chamber opens noiselessly. Sieglinde comes out in a white garment and advances softly but quickly towards the hearth.

Sieglinde   Art asleep?

Siegmund   Who steals this way?
Joyfully surprised.

Sieglinde   'Tis I: listen to me!
With stealthy haste.   In sleep profound lies Hunding;
                                  The draught that I mixed him I drugged.
                                  Use to good purpose the night!

Siegmund   Thou here, all is well!
Ardently interrupting.

Sieglinde   I have come to show thee a weapon;

O couldst thou make it thine!
I then might call thee
First among heroes,
For only by him
Can it be won.
O hearken: heed what I tell thee!
Here Hunding's kinsmen
Sat in the hall,
Assembled to honour his wedding.
He took as his wife,
Against her will,
One who was bartered by thieves.
Sad I sat there
Through their carousing.
A stranger entered the hall,
An old and grey-coated man.
So slouched was his hat
That one of his eyes was hidden;
But the other flashed
So that all feared it:
Overwhelming
Its menace they found;
I alone
Suffered, when looked on,
Sweet pain, sad delight,
Sorrow and solace in one.
On me glancing,
He scowled at the others,
As he swung a sword in his hands.
This sword he plunged
In the ash-tree's stem,
To the hilt driving it home.
The weapon he gains in guerdon
Who draws it from its place.
Though sore they struggled,
Not one of the heroes
Could win the weapon for his;
Coming, going,
The guests essayed it,
The strongest tugged at the steel;
Not an inch it stirred in the stem;
In silence yonder it cleaves.

I knew then who he was
That in sorrow greeted me.
I know too
Now for whom
The sword was stuck in the tree.
O might I to-day
Find here the friend
Brought from afar
By a woman's woe!
Then all I have suffered
In sorrow untold,
All scorn and all shame
In anger endured—
All would avenged be,
Sweetly atoned for—
Regained fully
The good I had lost;
For mine I should win
All I had wept for,
Could I but find the dear friend,
And clasp him close in my arms!

Siegmund
Embracing Sieglinde with passionate ardour.

Dear woman, that friend
Holds thee at last,
Both woman and sword are his.
Here in my breast
Burns hot the oath
That welds us twain into one.
For all that I sought
I see now in thee,
In thee all
That once failed me I find.
Thou wert despised,
My portion was pain;
I was an outlaw,
Dishonoured wert thou;
Sweet revenge beckons,
Bids us be joyful;
I laugh
From sheer fulness of joy,
Holding thee, love, in my arms thus,
Feeling the beat of thy heart!

The outer door swings open.

Sieglinde   Ha, who went? Who entered there?
With a start of alarm tears herself away.

The door remains open. Outside a glorious spring night. The full moon shines in, throwing its bright light on the pair, so that they can suddenly see one another quite plainly.

Siegmund   No one went—
In soft ecstasy.   But one has come:
                                        Laughing the spring
                                        Enters the hall!

He draws Sieglinde with tender force on to the couch, so that she sits beside him. The moon shines more and more brightly.

                                        Winter storms have yielded
                                        To May's sweet moon,
                                        And mild and radiant
                                        Sparkles the spring.
                                        On balmy breezes
                                        Light and lovely,
                                        Weaving wonders,
                                        Soft she sways.
                                        Through field and forest
                                        She is breathing;
                                        Wide and open
                                        Laughs her eye;
                                        When blithe the birds are singing
                                        Sounds her voice;
                                        Fragrant odours
                                        She exhales;
                                        From her warm blood blossom flowers
                                        Welcome and joyous.
                                        Shoot and bud,
                                        They wax by her aid.
                                        With tender weapons armed,
                                        She conquers the world.
                                        Winter and storm yield
                                        To the strong attack.
                                        No wonder that, beaten boldly,
                                        At last the door should have opened,
                                        Which, stubborn and stiff,

Was keeping her out.
To find her sister
Hither she came;
By love has spring been allured;
Within our bosoms
Buried she lay;
Now glad she laughs to the light.
The bride who is sister
Is freed by the brother;
In ruin lies
What held them apart.
Loud rejoicing,
They meet and greet;
Lo! Love is mated with spring!

Sieglinde

Thou art the spring
That I used to pine for,
When pinched by the winter frost;
My heart hailed thee friend
With bliss and with fear,
When thy first glance fell on me sweetly
All I had seen appeared strange;
Friendless were my surroundings;
I never seemed to have known
Any one who came nigh.
Thee, however,
Straightway I knew,
And I saw thou wert mine
When I beheld thee:
What I hid in my heart,
All I am,
Clear as the day
Dawned to my sight
Like tones to the ear
Echoing back,
When, upon my frosty desert,
My eyes first beheld a friend.

She hangs enraptured on his neck, and looks him close in the face.

Siegmund
Transported.

O rapture most blissful!
Woman most blest!

Sieglinde
Close to his eyes.

O let me, closer
And closer clinging,
Discern more clearly
The sacred light
That from thine eyes
And face shines forth,
And so sweetly sways every sense!

Siegmund

The May-moon's light
Falls on thy face
Framed by masses
Of waving hair.
What snared my heart
'Tis easy to guess:
My gaze on loveliness feasts.

Sieglinde
Pushing the hair back from his brow, regards him with astonishment.

How broad and open
Is thy brow!
Blue-branching the veins
In thy temples entwine.
I hardly can endure
My burden of bliss.—
Of something I am reminded:—
The man I first saw to-day
Already I have seen!

Siegmund

A dream of love
I too recall;
I saw thee there
And yearned for thee sore!

Sieglinde

The stream has shown me
My imaged face—
Again I see it before me;
As in the pool it arose
It is reflected by thee.

Siegmund

Thine is the face
I hid in my heart.

Sieglinde
Quickly averting her gaze.

O hush! That voice!
O let me listen!
These tones as a child
Surely I heard—
But no! I heard the sound lately,
When, calling in the wood,
My voice re-echoing rang.

Siegmund

To sweet and melodious
Music I listen!

Sieglinde
Gazing into his eyes again.

And ere now thy glowing
Eye have I seen:
The old man whose glance
Solaced my grief,
When he greeted me had that eye—
I knew him
Because of his eye,
And almost addressed him as father.

After a pause.

Art thou Wehwalt in truth?

Siegmund

If dear to thee,
Wehwalt no more;
My sway is o'er bliss not sorrow!

Sieglinde

And Friedmund does not
Fit with thy fortunes.

Siegmund

Choose thou the name
Thou wouldst have me be known by:
Thy choice will also be mine!

Sieglinde

The name of thy father was Wölfe?

Siegmund

A wolf to the fearful foxes!
But he whose eye
Shone with the brightness
Which, fairest one, shines in thine own,
Was named—Wälse of old.

Sieglinde
Beside herself.

Was Wälse thy father,
And art thou a Wälsung?—
Stuck was for thee
His sword in the stem?—
Then let my love call thee
What it has found thee;
Siegmund
Shall be thy name.

Siegmund
Springs up.

Siegmund call me
For Siegmund am I!
Be witness this sword
I grasp without shrinking!
That I should find it
In sorest need
Wälse foretold.
I grasp it now!
Love the most pure
In utmost need,
Passionate love,
Consuming desire
Burning bright in my breast,
Drive to deeds and death!
Nothung! Nothung!
That, sword, is thy name.
Nothung! Nothung!
Conquering steel!
Show me thy sharp
And sundering tooth:
Come forth from thy scabbard to me!

He draws the sword with a violent effort from the stem of the tree and shows it to the amazed and enraptured Sieglinde.

Siegmund the Wälsung
Thou dost see!
As bride-gift
He brings thee this sword;
With this he frees
The woman most blest;
He bears thee
From the house of his foe.
Far from here

Siegmund the Wälsung Thou dost see!
As bride-gift He brings thee this sword;

                                        Follow thou him:
                                        Forth to the laughing
                                        House of the spring;
                                        Thy shield be Nothung, the sword,
                                        When Siegmund is captive to love!

He throws his arm round her so as to draw her forth with him.

Sieglinde   Art thou Siegmund
Delirious with excitement, tears   Standing before me,
herself away and stands before him.   Sieglinde am I
                                        Who longed for thee;
                                        Thy own twin-sister
                                        As well as the sword thou hast won!

She throws herself on his breast.

Siegmund   Bride and sister
                                        Be to thy brother—
                                        So Wälsungs shall flourish for aye!

He draws her to him with fervent passion. The curtain falls quickly.

THE SECOND ACT

A wild, mountainous spot. In the background a gorge rises from below to a high ridge of rocks, from which the ground slopes down again towards the front. Wotan, in full armour, carrying his spear. Before him Brünnhilde as a Valkyrie, also fully armed.

Wotan	Go bridle thy steed,
	Valorous maid!
	Bitter strife
	Soon will break forth;
	Brünnhilde, storm to the fray
	And cause the Wälsung to win!
	Hunding choose for himself
	Where to bide:
	No place in Walhall has he.
	So up and to horse!
	Haste to the field!
Brünnhilde	Hojotoho! Hojotoho!
Ascends the height on the right,	Heiaha! Heiaha!
shouting and springing from rock	Hojotoho! Hojotoho!
to rock.	Heiaha! Heiaha!
	Hojotoho! Hojotoho!
	Hojotoho! Hojotoho!
	Heiaha! Hojoho!

She pauses on a high peak, looks down into the gorge and calls back to Wotan.

                                      I warn thee, Father,
                                      See to thyself;
                                      Stern the strife
                                      That is in store:
                                      Here comes Fricka, thy wife,
                                      Drawn hither in her car by her rams,
                                      Swinging the golden
                                      Scourge in her hand!
                                      The wretched beasts

Brunnhilde

Are groaning with fear;
And how the wheels rattle!
Hot she hastes to the fray.
Such strife as this
No strife is for me,
Though I love boldly waged
Strife 'twixt men.
The battle alone thou must brave;
I go; thou art left in the lurch!
Hojotoho! Hojotoho!
Heiaha! Heiaha!
Hojotoho! Hojotoho!
Heiaha! Heiaha!
Hojotoho! Hojotoho!
Hojotoho! Hojotoho!
Heiaha! Ha!

She disappears behind the mountain peak at the side. Fricka, in a car drawn by a pair of rams, has driven up the gorge to the mountain ridge, where she suddenly stops, alights and strides angrily towards Wotan in the foreground.

Wotan
Aside, when he sees Fricka approaching

The usual storm!
The usual strife!
But I must act with firmness

Fricka
Moderating her pace as she approaches, and confronting Wotan with dignity.

All alone among the hills
I seek thee, where thou dost hide
Fearing the eyes
Of thy wife,
That help in need thou may'st promise.

Wotan

Let Fricka tell
Her trouble in full.

Fricka

I have heard Hunding's cry,
For vengeance calling on me;
As wedlock's guardian
I gave ear:
My word passed
To punish the deed
Of this impious pair
Who boldly wrought him the wrong.

Wotan	Have this pair then
	Done such harm,
	Whom spring united in love?
	'Twas love's sweet magic
	That lured them on;
	None pays for love's might to me.

Fricka	How dull and how deaf thou wouldst seem!
	As though thou wert not aware
	That it is wedlock's
	Holy oath
	Profaned so rudely I grieve for.

Wotan	Unholy
	Hold I the bond
	That binds unloving hearts;
	Nor must thou
	Imagine that I
	Will restrain by force
	What transcends thy power;
	For where bold natures are stirring
	I urge them frankly to strife.

Fricka	Deeming thus laudable
	Wedlock's breach,
	Pray babble more nonsense
	And call it holy
	That shame should blossom forth
	From bond of a twin-born pair!
	I shudder at heart,
	My brain reels and whirls.
	Sister embraced
	As bride by the brother—
	Who has ever heard
	Of brother and sister as lovers?

Wotan	Thou hearest it now!
	Be taught by this
	That a thing may be
	Which has never befallen before.
	That those two are lovers

Thou must admit;
So take advice and be wise!
Thy blessing surely
Will bring to thee gladness,
If thou wilt, laughing on love,
Bless Siegmund and Sieglinde's bond.

Fricka
With a burst of deep indignation.

Then nothing to thee
Are the gods everlasting
Since the wild Wälsungs
Won thee for father?
I speak plainly—
Is that thy thought?
The holy and high
Immortals are worthless;
And all that once
Was esteemed is thrown over;
The bonds thou didst bind
By thyself now are broken;
Heaven's hold
Is loosed with a laugh,
That this twin-born pair, unimpeded,
The fruit of thy lawless love,
May in wantonness flourish and rule!
But why wail over
Wedlock and vows,
Since by thee the first they are scorned!
The faithful wife
Betrayed at each turn,
Lustfully longing
Wander thy glances;
Thine eyes scan
Each hollow and height
As thy fickle fancy allures thee,
While grief is gnawing my heart.
Heavy of soul
I had to endure it,
When to the fight
With the graceless maidens
Born out of wedlock,
Forth thou hast fared;
For, thy wife still holding in awe,

Frika approaches in Anger

Thou didst give her as maids
The Valkyrie band
To obedience bound,
Even Brünnhilde, bride of thy Wish.
But now that new names
Afford thee new pleasure,
And Wälse, wolfish, in
Forests has wandered;
Now that to bottomless
Shame thou hast stooped,
And a pair of mortals
Hast vilely begotten—
Now thy wife at the feet
Of whelps of a wolf thou dost fling!
Come finish thy work!
Fill the cup full!
Mock and trample now the betrayed one!

Wotan
Quietly.

Thou couldst not learn,
Though I might teach thee;
To thee there is nothing plain
Till day has dawned on the deed,
Wonted things
Thou alone canst conceive,
Whereas my spirit broods
On things not yet brought forth.
Listen, woman!
Some one we need,
A hero gods have not shielded,
And who is not bound by their law.
So alone
Were he fit for the deed
Which no god can accomplish,
Yet which must be done for the gods.

Fricka

With sayings dark
Thou fain wouldst deceive me!
What deed by hero
Could be accomplished
That was beyond the strength of the gods,
By whose grace alone he is strong?

Wotan	Then his own heart's courage Counts not at all?
Fricka	Who breathed their souls into men? Who opened their eyes, that they see? Behind thy shield Strong they appear; With thee to goad them, Upward they strive; Those men that thou praisest, 'Tis thou who spurrest them on. With falsehoods fresh Thou wouldst fain delude me, With new devices Thou wouldst evade me; Thou shalt not shelter The Wälsung from me; He lives only through thee, And is bold through thee alone.
Wotan *With emotion.*	He grew unaided In grievous distress; My shield sheltered him not.
Fricka	Then shield him not to-day; Take back the sword That thou hast bestowed.
Wotan	The sword?
Fricka	Yes, the sword, The magic sword Sudden and strong That thou gavest to thy son.
Wotan *Unsteadily.*	Nay, Siegmund won it Himself in his need.

From here Wotan's whole attitude expresses an ever-deepening uneasiness and gloom.

Fricka
Continuing passionately.

Both conquering sword
And the need came from thee.
Wouldst thou deceive me
Who, day and night,
At thy heels follow close?
For him thou didst strike
The sword in the stem;
Thou didst promise him
The peerless blade.
Canst thou deny
That thy cunning it was
Which led him where it lay hid?

Wotan makes a wrathful gesture. Fricka goes on more and more confidently as she sees the impression produced on him.

The Gods
Do not battle with bondsmen;
The free but punish transgressors.
Against thee, my peer,
Have I waged war,
But Siegmund is mine as my slave.

Another violent gesture from Wotan, who then seems to succumb to the feeling of his own powerlessness.

Shall thy eternal
Consort obey one
Who calls thee master
And bows as thy slave?
What! Shall I be
Despised by the basest,
To the lawless a spur,
A scoff to the free?
My husband cannot desire me,
A goddess, to suffer such shame!

Wotan
Gloomily.

What then wouldst thou?

Fricka

Shield not the Wälsung.

Wotan
in a muffled voice.

His way let him go.

Fricka	Thou wilt grant him no aid, When to arms the avenger calls?
Wotan	I shield him no more.
Fricka	Seek not to trick me; Look in my eyes! The Valkyrie turn from him too.
Wotan	The Valkyrie free shall choose.
Fricka	Not so; she but acts To accomplish thy will; Give order that Siegmund die.
Wotan *After a violent internal struggle*	Nay, slay him I cannot, He found my sword!
Fricka	Remove thou the magic, And shatter the blade: Swordless let him be found.
Brünnhilde *Is heard calling from the heights.*	Heiaha! Heiaha! Hojotoho! Heiaha! Heiaha! Heiohotojo! Hotojoha!
Fricka	Thy valorous maiden comes; Shouting, hither she rides.
Wotan	For Siegmund I called her to horse.

Brünnhilde appears with her horse on the rocky path to the right. When she sees Fricka she stops abruptly and, during the following, slowly and silently leads her horse down the path. She then puts it in a cave.

Fricka	By her shield to-day Be guarded the honour Of thy eternal spouse! Derided by men,

Brünnhilde slowly and silently leads her horse
down the path to the cave.

Shorn of our power,
Perish and pass would the Gods
If thy valiant maid
Avenged not to-day
My sacred and sovereign right.
The Wälsung falls for my honour.
Does Wotan now pledge me his oath?

Wotan   Take the oath!
Throwing himself on to a rocky seat in terrible dejection.

Fricka strides towards the back, where she meets Brünnhilde and halts for a moment before her.

Fricka
Warfather
Waits for thee;
He will instruct thee
How the lot is decreed!

She drives off quickly.

Brünnhilde
Comes forward anxious and wondering to Wotan, who leaning back on his rocky seat, is brooding gloomily.

Ill closed
The fight, I fear;
Fricka laughs at the outcome!
Father, what news
Hast thou to tell me?
Sad thou seemest and troubled!

Wotan
Dropping his arm helplessly and sinking his head on his breast.

By self-forged fetters
I am bound,
I, least free of all living!

Brünnhilde
I know thee not thus:
What gnaws at thy heart?

Wotan
His expression and gestures working up from this point, to a fearful outburst.

O sacrilege vile!
O grievous affront
Gods' despair!
Gods' despair!

Infinite wrath!
Woe without end!
Most sorrowful I of all living!

Brünnhilde
Alarmed, throws her shield, spear and helmet from her and kneels with anxious affection at his feet.

Father! Father!
Tell me what ails thee?
With dismay thou art filling thy child!
Confide in me
For I am true;
See, Brünnhilde begs it!

She lays her head and hands with tender anxiety on his knees and breast.

Wotan
Looks long in her eyes, then strokes her hair with involuntary tenderness. As if coming out of a deep reverie, he at last begins, very softly.

What if, when uttered,
Weaker it made
The controlling might of my will?

Brünnhilde
Very softly.

To Wotan's will thou speakest
When thou speakest to me?
What am I
If I am not thy will?

Wotan
Very softly.

What never to any was spoken
Shall be unspoken now and for ever.
Myself I speak to,
Speaking to thee.

In a low, muffled voice.

When young love grew
A waning delight,
'Twas power my spirit craved;
By rash and wild
Desires driven on,
I won myself the world.
Unknown to me
Dishonest my acts were;
Bargains I made

Father! Father! Tell me what ails thee?

Wherein hid mishap,
Craftily lured on by Loge,
Who straightway disappeared.
Yet I could not leave
Love altogether;
When grown mighty still I desired it.
The child of night,
The craven Nibelung,
Alberich, broke from its bond.
All love he forswore,
And procured by the curse
The gleaming gold of the Rhine,
And with it measureless might.
The ring that he wrought
I stole by my cunning,
But I restored it not
To the Rhine;
It paid the price
Of Walhall's towers:
The home the giants had built me,
From which I commanded the world.
She who knows all
That ever was,
Erda, the holy,
All-knowing Wala,
Warned me touching the ring:
Prophesied doom everlasting.
Of this doom I was fain
To hear further,
But silent she vanished from sight.
Then my gladness of heart was gone,
The god's one desire was to know.
To the womb of the earth
Downward then I went:
By love's sweet magic
Vanquished the Wala,
Troubled her wisdom proud,
And compelled her tongue to speak.
Tidings by her I was told;
And with her I left a fair pledge:
The world's wisest of women

                                               Bore me, Brünnhilde, thee.
With eight sisters
Fostered wert thou,
That ye Valkyries
Might avert the doom
Which the Wala's
Dread words foretold:
The gods' ignominious ending.
That foes might find us
Strong for the strife,
Heroes I got ye to gather.
The beings who served us
As slaves aforetime,
The men whose courage
Aforetime we curbed:
Who through treacherous bonds
And devious dealings
Were bound to the gods
In blindfold obedience—
To kindle these men
To strife was your duty,
To drive them on
To savage war,
That hosts of dauntless heroes
Might gather in Walhall's hall.

Brünnhilde

And well filled surely thy halls were;
Many a one I have brought.
We never were idle,
So why shouldst thou fear?

Wotan
His voice muffled again.

Another ill—
Mark what I say—
Was by the Wala foretold!
Through Alberich's hosts
Doom may befall us;
A furious grudge
Alberich bears me;
But now that my heroes
Make victory certain
I defy the hosts of the night.
Only if he won

The ring again from me,
Walhall were forfeit for ever.
Used by him alone
Who love forswore
Could the runes of the ring
Bring doom
To the mighty gods,
And shame without end.
My heroes' valour
He would pervert,
Would stir to strife
The bold ones themselves,
And with their strength
Wage war upon me.
So, alarmed, I resolved
To wrest the ring from the foeman.

In a low voice. I once paid Fafner,
One of the giants,
With gold accurst
For work achieved.
Fafner guards now the hoard
For which his own brother he slew.
The ring I must needs recover
With which his work I rewarded.
But I cannot strike one
By treaties protected;
Vanquished by him
My valour would fail.
These are the bonds
That bind my power;
I, who by treaties am lord,
To my treaties also am slave.
But what I dare not
One man may dare—
A hero never
Helped by my favour,
To me unknown
And granted no grace,
Unaware,
Bidden by none,
Constrained thereto
By his own distress—

                                He could achieve
                                What I must not do:
                                The deed I never urged,
                                Though it was all my desire.
                                But, alas! how to find
                                One to fight me, the god,
                                For my good—
                                Most friendly of foes!
                                How fashion the free one
                                By me unshielded,
                                In his proud defiance
                                Most precious to me?
                                How get me the other
                                Who, not through me,
                                But of himself
                                Will perform my will?
                                O woe of the gods!
                                Horrible shame!
                                Soul-sick am I
                                Of seeing myself
                                In all I ever created.
                                The other whom I so long for,
                                That other I never find.
                                The free by themselves must be fashioned,
                                All that I fashion are slaves!

Brünnhilde   But the Wälsung, Siegmund,
                                Works for himself.

Wotan   Wild I roamed
                                In the woodland with him,
                                Ever against the gods
                                Goading him to rebel.
Slowly and bitterly.   Now, when the gods seek vengeance,
                                Shield he has none but the sword
                                Given to him
                                By the grace of a god.
                                Why did I try
                                To trick myself vainly?
                                How easily Fricka
                                Found out the fraud!

	She read my inmost Heart to my shame. I must bend my will to her wishes.
Brünnhilde	Of victory wouldst Siegmund deprive?
Wotan	I have handled Alberich's ring, Loth to let the gold go. The curse that I fled Is following me: I must always lose what I love most, Slay what my heart holds dearest, Basely betray All those who trust.
His gestures, at first those of terrible grief end by expressing despair.	Pale then and pass Glory and pomp, Godhead's resplendent, Glittering shame! In ruins fall The fabric I built! Ended is my work; I wait but one thing more: The downfall— The downfall!
He pauses thoughtfully.	And for the downfall Schemes Alberich! Now I see The sense hidden In the strange, wild words of the Wala: "When the gloomy foe of love Gets a son in his wrath, The high gods' doom Shall be at hand!" Not long ago A rumour I heard That the dwarf had won a woman, By gold gaining her grace. A woman bears Hate's bitter fruit;

	The child of spite
	Grows in her womb;
	This marvel befell
	The man who loved not;
	But I, the loving wooer,
	Have never begotten the free.
Rising in bitter wrath.	Accept thou my blessing,
	Nibelung son!
	I leave to thee
	What I loathe with deep loathing:
	The hollow pomp of the gods.
	Consume it with envious greed!
Brünnhilde	O say! tell me
Alarmed.	What task is thy child's?
Wotan	Fight, faithful to Fricka;
Bitterly.	Wedlock and vows defend!
	What she desires
	Is also my choice,
	For what does my own will profit,
	Since it cannot fashion a free one?
	For Fricka's slaves
	Do battle henceforth!
Brünnhilde	Ah repent,
	And take back thy word!
	Thou lovest,
	And fain, I know,
	Wouldst have me shelter the Wälsung.
Wotan	Siegmund thou shalt vanquish,
	And fight so that Hunding prevails.
	Ward thyself well
	And doughtily do,
	Bring all thy boldness
	To bear on the field;
	A strong sword
	Swings Siegmund;
	Undismayed he will fight!

Brünnhilde   He whom thou still
Hast taught me to love,
He whose courage high
To thy heart was so precious—
I will shield him in spite of
Thy wavering word!

Wotan   Ha, daring one!
Floutest thou me?
Who art thou—who but the choiceless,
Blind slave of my will?
I have sunk so low
By showing my mind,
That the creature made by me
Holds me in scorn.
Dost thou, child, know my wrath?
If ever its awful
Lightning struck thee
Then quail wouldst thou indeed!
Within my bosom
Burns enough rage
To lay waste
In dread ruin a world
That once wore nothing but smiles.
Woe to him whom it strikes!
Dear the price he would pay!
So be advised,
Call it not forth
But carry out my commands.
Cut down Siegmund!
That is the Valkyrie's task.

He storms away and disappears among the rocks to the left.

Brünnhilde   Warfather
Stands for a long time dazed   Oft have I seen
and alarmed.   Enraged, but never once like this!
She stoops down sadly, takes up her armour and puts it on again.

How heavy
My armour feels!
And it felt so light

Brünnhilde stands for a long time, dazed and alarmed

	When gladly I fought!
	I fight afraid.
	Evil is my cause!
She gazes thoughtfully before her.	Woe! My Wälsung!
	With sorrow sore
She turns slowly towards the back.	Must the faithful one falsely forsake thee!

On reaching the rocky pass, Brünnhilde, looking down into the gorge, perceives Siegmund and Sieglinde. She watches them for a moment, then turns into the cave where her horse is, so that she is completely hidden from the audience. Siegmund and Sieglinde appear on the pass, Sieglinde hurrying in front. Siegmund tries to stop her.

Siegmund

Wait here and rest;
Tarry a while!

Sieglinde

Farther! Farther!

Siegmund
Embraces her with tender force, straining her to him.

No farther now!
O linger, woman most sweet!
From bliss when most blissful
Breaking away,
In headlong haste
Far thou hast fled,
So fleet that I lagged behind:
Through wood and field,
Over cliff and scaur,
Voiceless, silent,
Speeding along,
Thy foot stopped for no call.

Sieglinde stares wildly before her.

Tarry a while!
Say but a word,
Ending this speechless dread!
See, thy brother
Holds thee, his bride:
Siegmund's comrade art thou!

Sieglinde
Gazes into his eyes with growing rapture, throws her arms passionately round his neck and remains so for some time. She then starts up in wild terror.

Away! Away!
Fly the profaned one!
Unholy

The clasp of her arm;
In shame, dishonoured,
This body died.
Fling it from thee,
Flee from the corpse!
The winds scatter her dust—
The foul one who loved one so fair!
When in his loving embrace
She rested in rapture pure,
And all the love of the man
Was hers who loved him alone—
When on holiest height,
When bliss was at sweetest,
And sense and soul
Were steeped in delight,
Hatred and loathing
Of hideous dishonour
Shook the disgraced one,
Filled her with fear—
The thought she once had obeyed.
Bridegroom unloving, unloved.
Leave the accurst one,
Far let her fly!
An outcast she is,
Bereft of grace!
Ah, I must leave
The purest of heroes;
I cannot be thine,
To sully thy glory:
Scorn to bring on the brother,
Shame to the rescuing friend!

Siegmund

For the shame and dishonour,
Pay the transgressor's blood!
No farther, then, flying,
Here let us wait him;
Here—here I shall slay him:
When Nothung's point
Shall pierce his heart,
All thy wrongs will be avenged!

Sieglinde
Starts up and listens.

Hark! The bugles!
Dost thou not hear?
All around,
Angry and shrill,
From wood and vale
Clamour their calls.
Hunding has wakened
From slumber deep;
Kinsmen and hounds
He summons together;
How the dogs howl,
Urged on hotly,
Loud-baying to heaven
Of the vows and the wedlock profaned!

Gazes before her as if gone crazed.

Where art thou, Siegmund?
Art thou still here,
Fervently loved one,
Beautiful brother?
Let thine eyes like stars
Shine again on me softly;
Turn not away
From the outcast woman's kiss!

She throws herself sobbing on his breast, and presently starts up in terror again.

Hark! O hark!
That is Hunding's horn!
With his hounds full force,
In haste he comes.
No sword helps
When the dogs attack:—
Throw it down, Siegmund!
Siegmund, where art thou?
Ha, there! I see thee now!
Horrible sight!
Eager-fanged
Are the bloodhounds for flesh;
Ah, what to them
Is thy noble air!
By the feet they seize thee
With terrible teeth;
Alas!
Thou fallest with splintered sword:—

>   The ash-tree sinks—
>   The trunk is rent!
>   Brother! My brother!
>   Siegmund—ha!

She falls fainting into his arms.

Siegmund   Sister! Belovèd!

He listens to her breathing, and, when convinced that she still lives, lets her slide down so that, as he himself sinks into a sitting posture, her head rests upon his knees. In this position both remain till the end of the following scene. A long silence, during which Siegmund bends over Sieglinde with tender concern, and presses a long kiss on her brow.

Brünnhilde, leading her horse, comes out of the cave and walks slowly and solemnly towards the front. She pauses and watches Siegmund from a distance, then advances slowly again and stops when she gets nearer. In one hand she carries her shield and spear, the other rest on her horse's neck, and thus she gravely stands looking at Siegmund.

Brünnhilde   Siegmund!
                                     Look on me
                                     Whom thou
                                     Must follow soon!

Siegmund   Who art thou, say,
Looking up at her.   That dost stand so fair and so stern?

Brünnhilde   Death-doomed are they
                                     Who look upon me;
                                     Who sees me
                                     Bids farewell to the light of life.
                                     On the battle-field only
                                     Heroes view me;
                                     He whom I greet
                                     Is chosen and must go.

Siegmund

Looks into her eyes with a long steadfast and searching gaze, then bows his head in thought and finally turns resolutely to her again.

>   When thou dost lead,
>   Whither follows the hero?

Brünnhilde with her horse, at the mouth of the cave

Brünnhilde	I lead thee To Wotan; The lot he has cast: To Walhall must thou come.
Siegmund	In Walhall's hall Wotan alone shall I find?
Brünnhilde	A glorious host Of heroes slain Will greet thee there With love holy and high.
Siegmund	Say if in Walhall Sojourns my father, Wälse.
Brünnhilde	His father there Will the Wälsung find.
Siegmund *Tenderly.*	Will any woman Welcome me there?
Brünnhilde	Wishmaidens Serve there serene: Wotan's daughter Wine will bring for thy cup.
Siegmund	High art thou And holy of aspect, O Wotan's child: But one thing tell me, divine one! The sister and bride, Shall she follow the brother? Will Siegmund find Sieglinde there?
Brünnhilde	Air of earth Still she must breathe here; Siegmund will find no Sieglinde there!

Siegmund
Bends tenderly over Sieglinde, kisses her softly on the brow, and turns again quietly to Brünnhilde.

         Then greet for me Walhall,
         Greet for me Wotan,
         Greet for me Wälse
         And all the heroes,
         Wishmaidens lovely
         Greet thou also,
         And tell them I will not come!

Brünnhilde
         Nay, having looked
         On the Valkyrie's face,
         Thou must follow her forth!

Siegmund
         Where Sieglinde dwells
         In weal or woe,
         There will Siegmund dwell also;
         My face grew not pale
         When I beheld thee:
         Thou canst not force me to go!

Brünnhilde
         Force thee can none
         While thou dost live;
         Fool, what will force thee is death
         Warning of death
         Is what I bring.

Siegmund
         What hero to-day
         Shall hew me down?

Brünnhilde
         Hunding's hand in the fight.

Siegmund
         Use threats more baleful
         Than blows from Hunding!
         Lurkest thou here
         Longing for strife,
         Fix on him for thy prey.
         I think it is he who will fall!

Brünnhilde　　　　　　　　　　　Nay, Wälsung,
　　　　　　　　　　　　　　　　　　Doubt not my word;
　　　　　　　　　　　　　　　　　　Thine is the death decreed.

Siegmund　　　　　　　　　　　　Knowest this sword?
　　　　　　　　　　　　　　　　　　Who gave the sword
　　　　　　　　　　　　　　　　　　Gave triumph sure:
　　　　　　　　　　　　　　　　　　With this sword I laugh at thy threats.

Brünnhilde　　　　　　　　　　　He whose it was
In a loud voice.　　　　　　　　　　Now dooms thee to death,
　　　　　　　　　　　　　　　　　　For the magic spell he withdraws!

Siegmund　　　　　　　　　　　　Hush! Alarm not
Vehemently.　　　　　　　　　　　The slumberer here!
In an outburst of grief he bends tenderly over Sieglinde.
　　　　　　　　　　　　　　　　　　Woe! Woe!
　　　　　　　　　　　　　　　　　　Woman most sweet!
　　　　　　　　　　　　　　　　　　Most sad and ill-starred of all true ones!
　　　　　　　　　　　　　　　　　　Against thee rages
　　　　　　　　　　　　　　　　　　The whole world in arms,
　　　　　　　　　　　　　　　　　　And I who was all thy defence,
　　　　　　　　　　　　　　　　　　For whom thou the world hast defied—
　　　　　　　　　　　　　　　　　　To think I cannot
　　　　　　　　　　　　　　　　　　Shield thee, but, beaten
　　　　　　　　　　　　　　　　　　In battle, thy trust must betray!
　　　　　　　　　　　　　　　　　　O shame on him
　　　　　　　　　　　　　　　　　　Who bestowed the sword,
　　　　　　　　　　　　　　　　　　And triumph now turns to scorn!
　　　　　　　　　　　　　　　　　　If I must fall thus,
　　　　　　　　　　　　　　　　　　I fare to no Walhall—
He bends low over Sieglinde　　　　Hella hold me for aye!
.

Brünnhilde　　　　　　　　　　　So little prizest thou
Moved.　　　　　　　　　　　　　Life everlasting?
Slowly and with hesitation.　　　　　All thy care
　　　　　　　　　　　　　　　　　　Is thy helpless wife
　　　　　　　　　　　　　　　　　　Who, sad and weary,
　　　　　　　　　　　　　　　　　　Heavily hangs in thy arms?
　　　　　　　　　　　　　　　　　　Precious only is she?

Siegmund
Looking up at her bitterly.

Though young and fair
Thou shinest to me,
In my heart I know thee
Cruel and cold!
Canst thou do nothing
But mock me, begone,
Malicious, merciless maid!
Or if thou must gloat
Upon my distress,
Then gloat and feast thyself full!
With my woe
Solace thy envious soul:—
But of Walhall's loveless raptures
Nothing more let me hear!

Brünnhilde

I see the distress
That is tearing thy heart;
The doomed hero's holy
Sorrow I feel.
Siegmund, thy wife be my charge,
Protected safely by me.

Siegmund

No other than I
While my wife is living shall guard her.
If death be my lot
I will slay the slumberer first!

Brünnhilde
With increasing emotion.

Wälsung! Madman!
Listen to me!
Entrust her to me
For the pledge's sake
That she carries of thee and thy love!

Siegmund
Drawing his sword.

This sword
That a true man received from a false—
This sword
That fails me when facing the foe;
Worthless when turned on the foe,
Will serve me when turned on the friend.

He points the sword at Sieglinde.

Two lives now
Laugh to thee here:

	Take them, Nothung,
	Envious steel!
	Take them with one fell stroke!
Brünnhilde	Forbear, Wälsung!
With a passionate outburst	Listen to me!
of sympathy.	Sieglinde spare thou,
	And Siegmund too shall be spared!
	'Tis thus decreed,
	Recast the lot is!
	Thou, Siegmund,
	Shalt be blest and prevail!
Horns are heard in the distance.	Hark to the horn!
	Prepare for the fray;
	Trust to the sword
	And strike without fear:
	Thy sword shall prove strong
	Thee the Valkyrie faithfully shields!
	Farewell, Siegmund,
	Hero most blest!
	On the field again I shall find thee.

She rushes away and disappears with her horse down a gorge on the right. Siegmund gazes after her joyful and exultant. The stage has gradually grown dark. Heavy storm-clouds have gathered in the background, and hide the cliffs, gorge, and rocky pass completely from view.

Siegmund	Charmèd slumber
Bending over Sieglinde, listens to	Softly soothes
her breathing.	The dear one's pain and grief.
	When the Valkyrie came, perchance
	She brought her this blissful repose;
	Else would the grimly fought fight
	Have terrified one in such woe.
	Lifeless seems she,
	And yet she lives;
	The sad one by smiling
	Dreams is caressed.
	In slumber lie soft
	Till the fight is won
	And peace shall end thy pain!

He lays her gently on the rocky seat and kisses her brow in farewell. Then, hearing Hunding's horn sound, he starts up with resolution.

	Thou who dost call,
	Arm for the fray;
	Thy dues in full
	Thou shalt have:
He draws his sword.	Nothung pays him his debt.

He hastens to the back and, on reaching the pass, immediately disappears in a dark thunder-cloud, from which, the next instant, a flash of lightning breaks.

Sieglinde
Begins to move uneasily in her dreams. Would but my father come back!
With the boy he still roams in the wood.
Mother! Mother!
I am afraid—
The strangers seem
So harsh and unfriendly!
Fumes that stifle—
Dense and black smoke—
Fierce are the flames,
And closer they flare—
On fire the house!
O help us, brother!
Siegmund! Siegmund!

She starts up. Violent thunder and lightning.
Siegmund! Ha!

She stares about her in growing terror. Almost the whole of the stage is veiled by black thunder-clouds. Hunding's horn is heard close at hand.

Hunding's Voice
From the mountain pass
in the background.

Wehwalt! Wehwalt!
Stand there and fight,
Or with the hounds I will hold thee!

Siegmund's Voice
From farther back in the gorge.

Where hidest thou,
That I have missed thee thus?
Halt, that I may find thee!

Sieglinde
Listening in terrible fear.

Hunding—Siegmund—
Could I but see them!

Hunding

Come hither, impious wooer!
Here by Fricka be slain!

Siegmund
Also from the pass now.

Thou thinkest me weaponless,
Coward, still.
Threat not with women!
Thyself now fight me,
Lest Fricka fail thee at need!
For see, from the tree
That grows by thy hearth
I drew undaunted the sword;
Come and try the taste of its steel!

Sieglinde
With all her strength.

Hold your hands, ye men there!
Strike me dead first!

She rushes towards the pass, but is suddenly dazzled by a light which flashes forth from above the combatants to the right, and staggers aside as if blinded.

Brünnhilde's Voice

Strike him, Siegmund!
Trust to the sword!

Brünnhilde appears in the glare of light, floating above Siegmund, and protecting him with her shield. Just as Siegmund is aiming a deadly blow at Hunding a glowing red light breaks through the clouds from the left, in which Wotan appears, standing over Hunding and holding his spear across in front of Siegmund.

Wotan's Voice

Back! Back from the spear!
In splinters the sword!

Brünnhilde with her shield recoils in terror before Wotan; Siegmund's sword breaks in splinters on the outstretched spear. Hunding plunges his sword into the disarmed man's breast. Siegmund falls down dead, and Sieglinde, who has heard his death-sigh, sinks to the ground as if lifeless. With Siegmund's fall the lights on both sides disappear. Dense clouds shroud all but the foreground in darkness. Through these Brünnhilde is dimly seen turning in wild haste to Sieglinde.

Brünnhilde

To horse, that I may save thee!

She lifts Sieglinde up quickly on to her horse, which is standing near the side ravine, and immediately disappears. Thereupon the clouds divide in the middle, so that Hunding, who has just drawn his sword out of Siegmund's breast, is distinctly seen. Wotan, surrounded by clouds, stands on a rock behind, leaning on his spear and gazing sorrowfully on Siegmund's body.

Wotan
To Hunding.

Begone, slave!
Kneel before Fricka;
Tell her that Wotan's spear
Has slain what mocked her might.
Go! Go!

Before the contemptuous wave of his hand Hunding falls dead to the ground. Suddenly breaking out in terrible anger.

But Brünnhilde!
Woe to the guilty one!
Woe to her
As soon as my horse
Shall overtake her in flight!

He vanishes with thunder and lightning. The curtain falls quickly.

THE THIRD ACT

On the top of a rocky mountain

On the right the stage is bounded by a pine-wood. On the left is the entrance to a cave, above which the rock rises to its highest point. At the back the view is quite open. Rocks of varying heights form the edge of the precipice. Clouds fly at intervals past the mountain peak as if driven by storm. Gerhilde, Ortlinde, Waltraute, and Schwertleite have taken up their position on the rocky peak above the cave. They are in full armour.

Gerhilde
On the highest point, calling towards the background, where a dense cloud is passing.

> Hojotoho! Hojotoho!
> Heiaha! Heiaha!
> Helmwige! Here!
> Guide hither thy horse!

Helmwige's Voice
At the back.

> Hojotoho! Hojotoho!
> Hojotoho! Hojotoho!
> Heiaha!

A flash of lightning comes from the cloud, showing a Valkyrie on horseback, on whose saddle hangs a slain warrior. The apparition, approaching the cliff, passes from left to right.

Gerhilde, Waltraute & Schwertleite
Calling to her as she draws near. Heiaha! Heiaha!

The cloud with the apparition vanishes to the right behind the wood.

Ortlinde
Calling into the wood.

> Thy stallion make fast
> By Ortlinde's mare;

Waltraute
Calling towards the wood.

Gladly my grey
Will graze by thy chestnut!

Who hangs at thy saddle?

Helmwige
Coming out of the wood.

Sintolt the Hegeling!

Schwertleite

Fasten thy chestnut
Far from the grey then;
Ortlinde's mare
Carries Wittig, the Irming!

Gerhilde
Descending a little towards the others

And Sintolt and Wittig
Always were foemen!

Ortlinde
Springs up and runs to the wood.

Heiaha! Heiaha!
The horse is kicking my mare!

Gerhilde
Laughing with Helmwige & Schwertleite

The heroes' feud
Makes foes of the horses!

Helmwige
Calling back into the wood.

Quiet, Brownie!
Pick not a quarrel.

Waltraute
On the highest point, where listening towards the right she has taken Gerhilde's place as watcher, calling towards the right-hand side of the background.

Hoioho! Hoioho!
Siegrune, come!
What keeps thee so long?

Siegrune's Voice
From the back on the right.

Work to do.
Are the others all there?

The Valkyries
In answer, their gestures, as well as a bright light behind the wood, showing that Siegrune has just arrived there.

Hojotoho! Hojotoho!
Heiaha! Heiaha!

Grimgerde's & Rossweisse's Voices
From the back on the left.

Hojotoho! Hojotoho!
Heiaha!

Waltraute
Towards the left.

Grimgerde and Rossweisse!

Gerhilde

Together they ride.

In a cloud which passes across the stage from the left, and from which lightning flashes, Rossweisse and Grimgerde appear, also on horseback, each carrying a slain warrior on her saddle.

Helmwige, Ortlinde & Siegrune
Have come out of the wood and wave their hands from the edge of the precipice to Rossweisse and Grimgerde, who disappear behind the wood.

We greet you, valiant ones!
Rossweiss' and Grimgerde!

Rossweisse's & Grimgerde's Voices

Hojotoho! Hojotoho!
Heiaha!

All The Other Valkyries

Hojotoho! Hojotoho!
Heiaha! Heiaha!

Gerhilde
Calling into the wood.

Your horses lead into
The wood to rest!

Ortlinde
Also calling into the wood.

Lead the mares far off
One from the other,
Until our heroes'
Anger is laid!

Helmwige
The others laughing.

The grey has paid
For the heroes' anger.

Rossweiss and Grimgerde
Coming out of the wood.

Hojotoho! Hojotoho!

The Valkyries

Be welcomed! Be welcomed!

Schwertleite

Went ye twain on one quest?

Grimgerde

No, singly we rode,
And met but to-day.

Rossweisse

If we all are assembled
Why linger longer?
To Walhall let us away,
Bringing to Wotan the slain.

Helmwige

We are but eight;
Wanting is one.

Gerhilde

By the brown-eyed Wälsung
Brünnhilde tarries.

Waltraute

Until she joins us
Here we must wait;
Warfather's greeting
Grim were indeed
If we returned without her!

Siegrune
On the look-out, calling towards the back.
To the others.

Hojotoho! Hojotoho!

This way! This way!
In hottest haste riding,
Hither she comes.

The Valkyries
All hasten to the look-out.

Hojotoho! Hojotoho!
Heiaha!
Brünnhilde, hei!

They watch her with growing astonishment.

Waltraute

See, she leads woodward
Her staggering horse.

Grimgerde

From swift riding
How Grane pants!

Rossweisse	No Valkyrie's flight Ever so fast was.
Ortlinde	What lies on her saddle?
Helmwige	That is no man!
Siegrune	'Tis a woman, see!
Gerhilde	Where found she the maid?
Schwertleite	Has she no greeting For her sisters?
Waltraute *Calling down very loudly.*	Heiaha! Brünnhilde! Dost thou not hear?
Ortlinde	From her horse Let us help our sister.

Helmwige and Gerhilde run to the wood, followed by Siegrune and Rossweisse.

The Valkyries	Hojotoho! Hojotoho! Heiaha!
Waltraute *Looking into the wood.*	To earth has sunk Grane the strong one!
Grimgerde	From the saddle swift She snatches the maid.
The Other Valkyries *Running into the wood.*	Sister! Sister! What has occurred?

The Valkyries all return to the stage; Brünnhilde accompanies them, leading and supporting Sieglinde.

Brünnhilde *Breathless.*	Shield me and help In dire distress!

The Valkyries	Whence rodest thou hither, Hasting so hard? Thus ride they only who flee.
Brünnhilde	I flee for the first time And am pursued: Warfather follows close.
The Valkyries *Terribly alarmed.*	Hast thou gone crazy? Speak to us! What? Pursued by Warfather? Flying from him?
Brünnhilde *Turns and looks out anxiously, then comes back.*	O sisters, spy From the rocky peak! Look north and tell me If Warfather nears!

Ortlinde and Waltraute spring up the peak to the look-out.

Quick! Is he in sight?

Ortlinde	A storm from the north Is nearing.
Waltraute	Darkly the clouds Congregate there.
The Valkyries	Warfather, riding His sacred steed, comes!
Brünnhilde	The wrathful hunter, He rides from the north; He nears, he nears, in fury! Save this woman! Sisters your help!
The Valkyries	What threatens the woman?
Brünnhilde	Hark to me quickly! Sieglinde this is,

Warfather follows close...

Save this woman!
Sisters, your help!

	Siegmund's sister and bride. Wotan his fury Against the Wälsungs has turned. He told me That to-day I must fail The brother in strife; But with my shield I guarded him safe, Daring the God, Who slew him himself with his spear. Siegmund fell; But I fled, Bearing his bride. To protect her And from the stroke Of his wrath to hide, I hastened, O my sisters, to you!
The Valkyries *Full of fear.*	O foolish sister, How mad thy deed! Woe's me! Woe's me! Brünnhilde, lost one! Mocked, disobeyed By Brünnhilde Warfather's holy command!
Waltraute *On the look-out.*	Darkness comes From the north like the night.
Ortlinde *On the look-out.*	Hither steering, Rages the storm.
Rossweisse, Grimgerde & Schwertleite	Wildly neighs Warfather's horse!
Helmwige, Gerhilde & Siegrune	Panting, snorting it comes!
Brünnhilde	Woe to the woman If here she is found, For Wotan has vowed The Wälsungs shall perish!

	The horse that is swiftest Which of you lends, That forth the woman may fly?
Siegrune	Wouldst have us too Madly rebel?
Brünnhilde	Rossweisse, sister, Wilt lend me thy racer!
Rossweisse	The fleet one from Wotan Never yet fled.
Brünnhilde	Helmwige, hear me!
Helmwige	I flout not our father.
Brünnhilde	Waltraute! Gerhilde! Give me your horse! Schwertleite! Siegrune! See my distress! Stand by me now Because of our love: Rescue this woman in woe!

Sieglinde
Who until now has been staring gloomily and coldly before her, starts up with a repellent gesture as Brünnhilde encircles her with a warm, protective embrace.

                                        Concern thyself not about me;
                                        Death is all that I crave.
                                        From off the field
                                        Who bade thee thus bear me?
                                        For there perchance
                                        By the selfsame weapon
                                        That struck down Siegmund
                                        I too had died,
                                        Made one with him
                                        In the hour of death.
                                        Far from Siegmund—
                                        Siegmund, from thee!
                                        O cover me, Death,

	From the sorrow!
	Wouldst thou not have me
	Curse thee for flying?
	Thou must hearken, maid, to my prayer:
	Pierce thou my heart with thy sword!
Brünnhilde	Live for the sake
Impressively.	Of thy love, O woman!
	Rescue the pledge
	Thou has gotten from him:
	The Wälsung's child thou shalt bear!
Sieglinde	Save me, ye bold ones!
Gives a violent start; suddenly her	Rescue my child!
face beams with sublime joy.	Shelter me, maidens,
	And strong be your shield!

An ever-darkening thunderstorm nears from the back.

Waltraute	The storm has drawn nigh
On the look-out.	
Ortlinde	Fly, all who fear it!
The Valkyries	Hence with the woman;
	Here she is lost:
	The Valkyries dare not
	Shield her from doom!
Sieglinde	Save me, O maid
On her knees before Brünnhilde.	Rescue the mother!
Brünnhilde	Away then, and swiftly!
Raising Sieglinde with sudden resolve.	Alone thou shalt fly.
	I—stay in thy stead,
	Victim of Wotan's anger.
	I will hold here
	The God in his wrath,
	Till I know thee past reach of his rage.
Sieglinde	Say, whither shall my flight be?

Brünnhilde	Which of you, sisters,
	Eastward has journeyed?
Siegrune	A forest stretches
	Far in the east;
	The Nibelung's hoard
	By Fafner thither was borne.
Schwertleite	There as a dread
	Dragon he sojourns,
	And in a cave
	Keeps watch over Alberich's ring.
Grimgerde	'Tis uncanny there
	For a woman's home.
Brünnhilde	And yet from Wotan's wrath
	Shelter sure were the wood;
	For he both fears
	And keeps far from the place.
Waltraute	Raging, Wotan
On the look-out.	Rides to the rock!
The Valkyries	Brünnhilde, hark!
	Like a storm-wind he comes!
Brünnhilde	Flee then swiftly,
Urgently.	Thy face to the east!
	Boldly enduring,
	Defy every ill—
	Hunger and thirst,
	Briar and stone;
	Laugh, whether gnawed
	By anguish or want!
	For one thing know
	And hold to always—
	The world's most glorious hero
	Hideth, O woman, thy sheltering womb!

There as a dread Dragon he sojourns,
And in a cave keeps watch over Alberich's ring.

Brünnhilde takes the pieces of Siegmund's sword from under her breast-plate and gives them to Sieglinde.

The splintered sword's pieces
Guard securely;
From the field where slain was
His father I brought them.
And now I name
Him who one day
The sword new-welded shall swing—
"Siegfried" rejoice and prevail!

Sieglinde
Greatly moved.

Sublimest wonder!
Glorious maid!
From thee high solace
I have received!
For him whom we loved
I save the beloved one.
May my thanks one day
Sweet reward bring!
Fare thou well!
Be blest by Sieglind' in woe!

She hastens away to the right in front. The rocky peak is surrounded by black thunder-clouds. A fearful storm rages from the back. A fiery glow increases in strength to the right.

Wotan's Voice

Stay, Brünnhilde!

Ortlinde and Waltraute
Coming down from the look-out.

The rock is reached
By horse and rider!

Brünnhilde, after following Sieglinde with her eyes for a while, goes towards the background, looks into the wood, and comes forward again fearfully.

The Valkyries

Woe, Woe! Brünnhilde!
Vengeance he brings!

Brünnhilde

Ah, sisters, help!
My courage fails!
His wrath will crush me
Unless ye ward off its weight.

The Valkyries
Fly towards the rocky point in fear,
drawing Brünnhilde with them.

This way, then, lost one!
Hide from his sight!
Cling closely to us,
And heed not his call!

They hide Brünnhilde in their midst and look anxiously towards the wood, which is now lit up by a bright fiery glow, while in the background it has grown quite dark.

          Woe! Woe!
          Raging, Wotan
          Swings from his horse!
          Hither hastes
         His foot for revenge!

Wotan
Comes from the wood in a terrible state of wrath and excitement and goes towards the Valkyries on the height, looking angrily for Brünnhilde.

          Where is Brünnhilde?
          Where is the guilty one?
          Would ye defy me
          And hide the rebel?

The Valkyries

Fearful and loud thy rage is!
By what misdeed have thy daughters
Vexed and provoked thee
To terrible wrath?

Wotan

Fools, would ye flout me?
Have a care, rash ones!
I know: Brünnhilde
Fain ye would hide.
Leave her, the lost one
Cast off for ever,
Even as she
Cast off her worth!

The Valkyries

To us fled the pursued one,
In her need praying for help,
Dismayed and fearful,
Dreading thy wrath.
For our trembling sister
Humbly we beg
That thy first wild rage be calmed.

Wotan

Weak-hearted
And womanish brood!
Is this your valour,
Given by me?
For this have I reared you
Bold for the fight,
Made you relentless
And hard of heart
That ye wild ones might weep and whine
When my wrath on a faithless one falls?
Learn, wretched whimperers,
What was the crime
Of her for whom
Ye are shedding those tears.
No one but she
Knew what most deeply I brooded;
No one but she
Pierced to the source of my being;
Through her deeds
All, I wished to be, came to birth.
This sacred bond
So completely she broke
That she defied me,
Opposing my will,
Her master's command
Openly mocked,
And against me pointed the spear
That she held from me alone.
Hearest, Brünnhilde?
Thou who didst hold
Thy helm and spear,
Grace and delight,
Life and name as my gift!
Hearing my voice thus accusing,
Dost hide from me in terror,
A coward who shirks her doom?

Brünnhilde
Steps out from the band of Valkyries, and humbly but with a firm step descends from the rocky peak until within a short distance from Wotan.

Here I am, Father,
Awaiting thy sentence!

Wotan	I – sentence thee not;
	Thou hast shaped thy doom for thyself.
	Through my will only
	Wert thou at all,
	Yet against my will thou hast worked;
	Thy part it was
	To fulfil my commands,
	Yet against me thou hast commanded;
	Wish-maid
	Thou wert to me,
	Yet thy wish has dared to cross mine;
	Shield-maid
	Thou wert to me,
	Yet against me raised was thy shield;
	Lot-chooser
	Thou wert to me:
	Against me the lot thou hast chosen;
	Hero-rouser
	Thou wert to me:
	Thou hast roused up heroes against me.
	What once thou wert
	Wotan has told thee:
	What thou art now,
	Demand of thyself!
	Wish-maid thou art no more;
	Valkyrie thou art no longer:—
	What now thou art
	For aye thou shalt be!
Brünnhilde	Thou dost cast me off?
Greatly terrified	Ah, can it be so?
Wotan	No more shall I send thee from Walhall
	To seek upon fierce
	Fields for the slain;
	With heroes no more
	Shalt thou fill my hall:
	When the high Gods sit at banquet,
	No more shalt thou pour
	The wine in my horn;
	No more shall I kiss

The mouth of my child.
Among heaven's hosts
Numbered no longer,
Outcast art thou
From the kinship of Gods;
Our bond is broken in twain,
And from my sight henceforth thou
now art banned.

The Valkyries
Leave their places in the excitement, and come a little farther down the rocks.
Woe's me! Woe!
Sister! O sister!

Brünnhilde

All that thou gavest
Thou dost recall?

Wotan

Conquering thee, one shall take all!
For here on the rock
Bound thou shalt be,
Defenceless in sleep,
Charmed and enchained;
The man who chances this way
And awakes her, shall master the maid.

The Valkyries
Come down from the height in great excitement, and in terrified groups surround Brünnhilde, who lies half kneeling before Wotan.
O stay, Father!
The sentence recall.
Shall the maiden droop
And be withered by man?
O dread one, avert thou
The crying disgrace:
For as sisters share we her shame.

Wotan

Have ye not heard
Wotan's decree?
From out your band
Shall your traitorous sister be banished,

The Ride of the Valkyries

> No more to ride
> Through the clouds her swift steed to the battle;
> Her maidenhood's flower
> Will fade away;
> Her grace and her favour
> Her husband's will be;
> Her husband will rule her
> And she will obey;
> Beside the hearth she will spin,
> To all mockers a mark for scorn.

Brünnhilde sinks with a cry to the ground. The Valkyries, horror-stricken, recoil from her violently.

> Fear ye her fate?
> Then fly from the lost one!
> Swiftly forsake
> And flee from her far!
> Let one but venture
> Near her to linger,
> Seek to befriend her,
> Defying my will—
> The fool shall share the same doom:
> I warn you, ye bold ones, well!
> Up and away!
> Hence, and return not!
> Get ye gone at a gallop,
> Trouble is rife else for you here!

The Valkyries   Woe! Woe!

Separate with a wild cry and rush into the wood.

Black clouds settle thickly on the cliff; a rushing sound is heard in the wood. From the clouds breaks a vivid flash of lightning, by which the Valkyries are seen packed closely together, and riding wildly away with loose bridles. The storm soon subsides; the thunder-clouds gradually disperse. In the following scene the weather becomes fine again and twilight falls, followed at the close by night.

Wotan and Brünnhilde, who lies stretched at his feet, remain behind alone. A long solemn silence.

Brünnhilde
Begins to raise her head a little, and, commencing timidly, gains confidence as she proceeds.

                Was the offence
                So shameful and foul
                That to such shame the offender should
                                be doomed?
                Was what I did
                So base and so vile
                That I must suffer abasement so low?
                Was the dishonour
                Truly so deep
                That it must rob me of honour for aye?

She raises herself gradually to a kneeling posture.
                O speak, Father!
                In my eye looking,
                Calming thy rage,
                Taming thy wrath,
                Explain why so dark
                This deed of mine
                That in thy implacable anger
                It costs thee thy favourite child!

Wotan   Ask of thy deed,
His attitude unchanged, gravely And that will show thee thy guilt!
and gloomily.

Brünnhilde   I but fulfilled
                               Wotan's command.

Wotan   By my command
                               Didst thou fight for the Wälsung?

Brünnhilde   Yea, lord of the lots,
                               So ran thy decree.

Wotan   But I took back
                               The order, changed the decree!

Brünnhilde   When Fricka had weaned
                               Thy will from its purpose;
                               In yielding what she desired
                               Thou wert a foe to thyself.

Wotan
Softly and bitterly.

I thought thou didst understand me,
And punished thy conscious revolt;
But coward and fool
I seemed to thee!
If I had not treason to punish
Thou wouldst be unworthy my wrath.

Brünnhilde

I am not wise,
But I knew well this one thing—
That thy love was the Wälsung's;
I knew that, by discord
Drawn two ways,
This one thing thou hadst forgotten.
The other only
Couldst thou discern—
What so bitterly
Wounded thy heart:
That Siegmund might not be shielded.

Wotan

And yet thou didst dare
To shield him, knowing 'twas so?

Brünnhilde
Beginning softly.

Because I the one thing
Had kept in my eye,
While by twofold desire
Divided wert thou,
Blindly thy back on him turning!
She who wards thy back
From the foe in the field,
She saw alone
What thou sawest not:—
Siegmund I beheld.
Bringing him doom
I approached;
I looked in his eyes,
Gave ear to his words.
I perceived the hero's
Bitter distress;
Loud the lament
Of the brave one resounded;
Uttermost love's

Most terrible pang,
Saddest of hearts
Defying all odds—-
With my ear I heard,
My eye beheld
That which stirred the heart in my breast
With trouble holy and strange.
Shamed, astonished,
Shrinking I stood.
Then all my thought
Was how I could serve him;
Triumph and death
To share with Siegmund—
That seemed, that only,
The lot I could choose!
Faithful to him
Who taught my heart this love,
And set me
By the Wälsung's side as friend—
Most faithful to him—
Thy word I disobeyed.

Wotan

So thou hast done
What I yearned so greatly to do—
What a twofold fate
Withheld from my desire!
So easy seemed to thee
Heart's delight in the winning,
When burning woe
In my heart flamed fierce,
When terrible anguish
Wrung my soul,
When, to save the world
That I loved, love's spring
In my tortured heart I imprisoned?
Against my own self
When I turned, to my torment,
From swooning pain
Arose in a frenzy,
When a wild longing
Burning like fire
The fearful design in me woke

Somewhat freely.   In the ruins of my own world
My unending sorrow to bury,
Thy heart was lapped
In blissful delight.
Trembling with rapture,
Drunken with joy,
Thy lips drank laughing
The draught of love,
While I drank of divine woe
Mixed with wormwood and gall.

Dryly and shortly.   By thy lightsome heart
Henceforth be guided:
From me thou hast turned away!
I must renounce thee;
Together no more
Shall we two whisper counsel;
Apart our paths lie,
Sundered for ever,
And so long as life lasts
I, the God, dare nevermore greet thee!

Brünnhilde
Simply.

Unfit was the foolish
Maid for thee,
Who, dazed by thy counsel,
Grasped not thy mind
When, to her, one counsel
Alone appeared plain—
To love what was loved by thee.
If I must forth
Where I shall not find thee,
If the fast-woven bond
Must be loosed,
And half thy being
Far from thee banished—
A half once thine and thine only,
O God, forget not that!—
Thy other self
Thou wilt not dishonour,
Dealing out shame
That will shame thee too;

Wotan

Thine own honour were lowered,
Were I a target for scorn!

The lure of love
Thou hast followed fain:
Follow the man
Who shall wield its might!

Brünnhilde

If I must go from Walhall,
No more in thy work be a sharer,
And if as my master
A man I must serve,
To braggart base
Abandon me not!
Not all unworthy
Be he who wins!

Wotan

With Wotan no part hast thou—
He cannot fashion thy fate.

Brünnhilde

By thee has been founded a race
Too glorious to bring forth a coward
One day must a matchless hero
From Wälsung lineage spring.

Wotan

Name not the Wälsungs to me!
Renouncing thee,
Them too I renounced;
Through envy they came to naught.

Brünnhilde

With an air of secrecy.

She who turned from thee
Rescued the race;
Sieglinde bears
Fruit holy and high;
In pain and woe
Beyond woe known to woman
She will bring forth
What in fear she hides!

Wotan

No shelter for her
Seek at my hand,
Nor for fruit that she may bear.

Brünnhilde

The sword she has kept
That thou gavest Siegmund.

Wotan
Violently.

And that I splintered with my spear.
Strive not, O maid,
My spirit to trouble!
Await thou the lot
Cast and decreed;
I cannot choose it or change!
But now I must forth,
Fare from thee far;
Too long I stay by thy side.
I must turn from thee,
As thou didst from me;
I must not even
Know thy desire;
Thy doom alone
I must see fulfilled!

Brünnhilde

And what is the doom
That I must suffer?

Wotan

In slumber fast
Thou shalt be locked;
Wife thou shalt be to the man
Who finds and wakes thee from sleep!

Brünnhilde
Falls on her knees.

If fettering sleep
Fast must bind me,
An easy prey
To the basest coward,
This one thing that in deep anguish
I plead for thou must accord!
O shield thou the sleeper
With soul-daunting terrors,

Firmly.

That by a dauntless
Hero alone
Here on the rock
I may be found!

Wotan

Too much thou askest—
Too big a boon!

Brünnhilde
Clasping his knees.

This one thing
Grant me, O grant me!
The child that is clasping
Thy knees crush dead;
Tread down thy dear one
And shatter the maid;
Let her body perish,
Pierced by thy spear,
But, cruel one, expose her not
To this crying shame!

With wild ecstasy.

O cause a fire
To burn at thy bidding,
With flame fiercely flaring
Girdle the rock,
And may its tongue lick,
And may its tooth eat
The coward who, daring, rashly
Approaches the terrible spot!

Wotan
Overcome and deeply stirred, turns quickly towards Brünnhilde, raises her from her knees and looks into her eyes with emotion.

Farewell, thou valiant,
Glorious child!
Thou the most holy
Pride of my heart,
Farewell! Farewell! Farewell!

Passionately.

Must we be parted?
Shall I never more
Give thee love's greeting?
Must thou no longer
Gallop beside me,
Nor bring me mead at banquet?
If I must lose thee,
Whom I have loved so,
The laughing delight of my eyes,
For thee there shall burn
A bridal fire brighter

A bridal fire brighter... Than ever yet burned for a bride!

Than ever yet burned for a bride!
Fiercely the flames
Shall flare round thy bed,
Flames dreadful, devouring,
Daunting all cowards;
Let cravens flee
From Brünnhilde's rock!
One only shall set the bride free,
One freer than I, the God!

Moved and enraptured, Brünnhilde sinks on the breast of Wotan, who holds her in a long embrace; then she throws back her head again, and, still embracing him, gazes into his eyes with emotion and awe.

Those eyes so lovely and bright
That oft with smiles I caressed,
Thy valour
With a kiss rewarding
When, sweetly lisped
By thy childlike mouth,
The praise of heroes I heard:
Those eyes so radiant and fair
That oft in storm on me shone,
When hopeless yearning
My heart was wasting,
And when the joy
Of the world I longed for,
While fears thronged thick around me–
Once more to-day
Gladdening me,
Let them take this kiss
Of fond farewell!
On happier mortal
May they yet shine;
On me, hapless immortal,
Must they close, and for ever!

He takes her head in both hands.

'Tis thus that the God
From thee turns:
He kisses thy Godhead away!

He kisses her long on the eyes, and with these closed she sinks back softly into his arms, unconscious. He carries her gently to a low mossy mound, and lays her there beneath the broad-spreading pine-tree which overshadows it. He gazes at her and closes her helmet; his eyes then rest on the form of the sleeper, which he completely

Loge! Loge! Appear!

covers with the great steel shield of the Valkyries. Having done so, he moves slowly away, turning to take one more sorrowful look. Then he strides with solemn resolve to the middle of the stage, and points his sword towards a large rock.

> Loge, hear!
> Hark to my word!
> I who found thee at first
> A fiery flame,
> And from whom thou didst vanish
> In wandering fire,
> I, who once bound,
> Bid thee break forth!
> Appear, flickering fire,
> Encircle the rock with thy flame!

He strikes the rock three times with his spear during the following.

> Loge! Loge! Appear!

A gleam of fire issues from the stone and gradually becomes a fiery glow; then flickering flames break forth. Soon wild, shooting flames surround Wotan, who, with his spear, directs the sea of fire to encircle the rock. It spreads towards the background, so that the mountain is surrounded by flame.

> Let none who fears
> The spear of Wotan
> Adventure across this fire!

He stretches out his spear as a ban, looks sorrowfully back at Brünnhilde, then moves slowly away, turning his head for a farewell gaze. Finally he disappears through the fire.

The Curtain Falls.

The Sleep of Brünnhilde

The Ring of the Nibelung
Volume 1

finis

AZILOTH BOOKS

Aziloth Books publishes a wide range of titles ranging from hard-to-find esoteric books - *Parchment Books* - to classic works on fiction, politics and philosophy - *Cathedral Classics*. Our newest venture is *Aziloth Books Children's Classics*, with vibrant new covers and illustrations to complement some of the world's very best children's tales. All our imprints are offered to the reader at a competitive price and through as many mediums and outlets as possible.

We are committed to excellent book production and strive, whenever possible, to add value to our titles with original images, maps and author introductions. With the premium on space in most modern dwellings, we also endeavour - within the limits of good book design - to make our products as slender as possible, allowing more books to be fitted into a given bookshelf area.

We are a small, approachable company and would love to hear any of your comments and suggestions on our plans, products, or indeed on absolutely anything.

Aziloth Books, Rimey Law, Rookhope, Co. Durham, DL13 2BL, England.
t: 01388-517600 e: info@azilothbooks.com w: www.azilothbooks.com

Parchment Books
AZILOTH

PARCHMENT BOOKS enshrines the concept of the oneness of all true religious traditions - that "the light shines from many different lanterns". Our list below offers titles from both eastern and western spiritual traditions, including Christian, Judaic, Islamic, Daoist, Hindu and Buddhist mystical texts, as well as books on alchemy, hermeticism, paganism, etc..

By bringing together such spiritual texts, we hope to make esoteric and occult knowledge more readily available to those ready to receive it. We do not publish grimoires or titles pertaining to the left hand path. Titles include:

The Prophet	Khalil Gibran
The Madman: His Parables & Poems	Khalil Gibran
Abandonment to Divine Providence	Jean-Pierre de Caussade
Corpus Hermeticum	G. R. S. Mead (trans.)
The Holy Rule of St Benedict	St. Benedict of Nursia
The Confession of St Patrick	St. Patrick
The Outline of Sanity	G. K. Chesterton
An Outline of Occult Science	Rudolf Steiner
The Dialogue Of St Catherine Of Siena	St. Catherine of Siena
Esoteric Christianity; Thought-Forms*	Annie Besant
The Teachings of Zoroaster	Shapurji A. Kapadia
The Spiritual Exercises of St. Ignatius	St. Ignatius of Loyola
Daemonologie	King James of England
A Dweller on Two Planets	Phylos the Thibetan
Bushido*	Nitobe Inazo
The Interior Castle	St. Teresa of Avila
Songs of Innocence & Experience*	William Blake
The Secret of the Rosary	St. Louis Marie de Montfort
From Ritual to Romance	Jessie L. Weston
The God of the Witches	Margaret Murray
Kundalini – an occult experience	George S. Arundale
The Kingdom of God is Within You	Leo Tolstoy
The Trial and Death of Socrates	Plato
A Textbook of Theosophy	Charles W. Leadbetter
Chuang Tzu: Daoist Teachings	Chuang Tzu
Practical Mysticism	Evelyn Underhill
Tao Te Ching (Lao Tzu's 'Book of the Way')	Tzu, Lao
The Most Holy Trinosophia	Le Comte de St.-Germain
Tertium Organum	P. D. Ouspensky
Totem and Taboo	Sigmund Freud
The Kebra Negast	E. A. Wallis Budge
Esoteric Buddhism	Alfred Percy Sinnett
Demian: the story of a youth	Hermann Hesse
Religio Medici	Thomas Browne
The Jefferson Bible	Thomas Jefferson
The Dhammapada	W. Wagiswara & K. Saunders

* with colour illustrations

Obtainable at all good online and local bookstores.
View Aziloth Books' full list at: www.azilothbooks.com

Cathedral Classics

CATHEDRAL CLASSICS hosts an array of classic literature, from erudite ancient tomes to avant-garde, twentieth-century masterpieces, all of which deserve a place in your home. All the world's great novelists are here, Jane Austen, Dickens, Conrad, Arthur Machen and Henry James, brushing shoulders with such disparate luminaries as Sun Tzu, Marcus Aurelius, Kipling, Friedrich Nietzsche, Machiavelli, and Omar Khayam. A small selection is detailed below:

Frankenstein	Mary Shelley
Herland; With Her in Ourland	Charlotte Perkins Gilman
The Time Machine; The Invisible Man	H. G. Wells
Three Men in a Boat	Jerome K Jerome
The Rubaiyat of Omar Khayyam	Omar Khayyam
A Study in Scarlet	Arthur Conan Doyle
The Sign of the Four	Arthur Conan Doyle
The Picture of Dorian Gray	Oscar Wilde
Flatland	Edwin A. Abbott
The Coming Race	Bulwer Lytton
The Adventures of Sherlock Holmes	Arthur Conan Doyle
The Great God Pan	Arthur Machen
Beyond Good and Evil	Friedrich Nietzsche
England, My England	D. H. Lawrence
The Castle of Otranto	Horace Walpole
Self-Reliance, & Other Essays (series1&2)	Ralph W. Emmerson
The Art of War	Sun Tzu
A Shepherd's Life	W. H. Hudson
The Double	Fyodor Dostoyevsky
To the Lighthouse; Mrs Dalloway	Virginia Woolf
The Sorrows of Young Werther	Johann W. Goethe
Leaves of Grass - 1855 edition	Walt Whitman
Analects	Confucius
Beowulf	Anonymous
Plain Tales From The Hills	Rudyard Kipling
The Subjection of Women	John Stuart Mill
The Rights of Man	Thomas Paine
Progress and Poverty	Henry George
Captain Blood	Rafael Sabatini
Captains Courageous	Rudyard Kipling
The Meditations of Marcus Aurelius	Marcus Aurelius
The Social Contract	Jean Jacques Rousseau
War is a Racket	Smedley D. Butler
The Dead	James Joyce
The Old Wives' Tale	Arnold Bennett
Letters Concerning the English Nation	Voltaire
Portrait of the Artist As a Young Man	James Joyce
Coningsby	Benjamin Disraeli

Obtainable at all good online and local bookstores.
View Aziloth Books' full list at: www.azilothbooks.com

AZILOTH BOOKS — CHILDREN'S Classics

Aziloth Books is passionate about bringing the very best in children's classic fiction to the next generation of book-lovers. We believe in the transforming power of children's books to encourage a life-long love of reading, and publish only the best authors and illustrators. With its original design and outstanding quality, our highly successful list has something to suit every age and interest. Titles include:

The Railway Children	Edith Nesbit
Anne of Green Gables	Lucy Maud Montgomery
What Katy Did	Susan Coolidge
Puck of Pook's Hill	Rudyard Kipling
The Jungle Books	Rudyard Kipling
Just So Stories	Rudyard Kipling
Alice Through the Looking Glass	Charles Dodgson
Alice's Adventures in Wonderland*	Charles Dodgson
Black Beauty	Anna Sewell
The War of the Worlds	H. G Wells
The Time Machine	H. G .Wells
The Sleeper Awakes	H. G. Wells
The Invisible Man	H. G. Wells
The Lost World	Sir Arthur Conan Doyle
Gulliver's Travels*	Jonathan Swift
Catriona (David Balfour)	Robert Louis Stevenson
The Water Babies	Charles Kingsley
The First Men in the Moon	Jules Verne
The Secret Garden	Frances Hodgson Burnett
A Little Princess	Frances Hodgson Burnett
Peter Pan*	J. M. Barrie
The Song of Hiawatha*	Henry W. Longfellow
Tales from Shakespeare	Charles and Mary Lamb
The Wonderful Wizard of Oz	L. Frank Baum
The Complete Grimm's Fairy Tales	Jacob & Wilhelm Grimm
The Wind in the Willows*	Kenneth Grahame

*with colour illustrations

Obtainable at all good online and local bookstores.
View Aziloth Books' full list at: www.azilothbooks.com